15 Strange Tales of Crime and Mystery

Also by Mario Milosevic

Novels
Claypot Dreamstance
The Coma Monologues
The Doctor and the Clown
Kyle's War
The Last Giant
Splitting
Terrastina and Mazolli

Collections
Entangled Realities (with Kim Antieau)
Labor Days
Miniatures

Poetry
Animal Life
Fantasy Life
Love Life

15 Strange Tales of Crime and Mystery

Mario Milosevic

Green Snake PUBLISHING

15 Strange Tales of Crime and Mystery
by Mario Milosevic

ISBN-13: 978-1-949644-12-8

The following stories have been previously published:
"Democracy" originally appeared in *Fiction River: Hidden in Crime*, 2015.
"Weedhead" originally appeared in *Pulp Empire*, 2011.
"Property Lines" originally appeared in *Alfred Hitchcock's Mystery Magazine*, March 2012.
"Parallel Moons" originally appeared in *Space and Time* #110, Spring 2010.
"The Universe of Death" originally appeared as an ebook from Green Snake Publishing, 2012 .
"The Clex Are Our Friends" originally appeared on *Daily Science Fiction*, June 14, 2011.
"They Taste Like Chicken" originally appeared as an ebook from Green Snake Publishing, 2011.
"The Last Last Meal" originally appeared as an ebook from Green Snake Publishing, 2011.
"The Visitor From the Dark Mountain" originally appeared in *Miniatures*, 2012.

Thanks to Nancy Milosevic

Cover photo by Kim Antieau

Published by Green Snake Publishing
www.greensnakepublishing.com

Contents

Democracy

My name is Robin Curtis. I came to the hot dry lands of eastern Oregon territory in 1870 and settled in a small town called Glory.

The town, if I may say, was not well-named. Glory consisted of shacks and some dirt roads. Several large ranches surrounded it, where rough-hewn cowboys raised cattle and where women such as myself, independent and prone to live life on my own terms, were somewhat tolerated, if not embraced.

My life in the east does not bear telling here. I would say only that it was less endurable, owing to the dominance of a husband prone to violence, than the dismal surroundings in the Oregon territory.

I was fortunate to have inherited, from a distant cousin, a parcel of land adjacent to Glory.

I came to the town to claim that land and to find a life on the frontier.

But I did not come as a woman.

Instead, I disguised myself. I wore men's clothes and cut my hair short and determined to present myself as a man, knowing it would protect me from the advances of males.

It worked. It helped, I may say, that my name could have been applied to both males and females. I went about town, tending to my business, and did not raise any suspicions.

Until election day.

Glory was in need of a new sheriff. The old one had been a drinker, and a lazy one to boot, and he was dismissed by the judge. Now two candidates had thrown their hats into the ring.

I knew both of them only a little.

Martin Cadwell was a young buck, only twenty-one, but with fire in his eyes. He wanted to protect the town from Natives and insure that no cow would ever be rustled again.

I liked him.

Noah Spencer was older, at least forty by my estimation, and had been sheriff in other frontier towns. His main concern was to keep the town free of undesirables. He promised to shoot anyone who so much as looked at him sideways.

I was not disposed to appreciate Mr. Spencer's qualities.

The town was evenly divided on the question of who should be the next sheriff. You could go into any drinking establishment, as I did, in the weeks before election, and hear heated arguments extolling the virtues of both candidates.

They had one debate, which attracted most of the town, my own interested self, included.

I listened carefully to both men. They were certainly eager to present their views to the townspeople. I found myself, inexplicably, finding less to admire in Mr. Cadwell and more to admire in Mr. Spencer.

This set my head spinning. Before long, I did not know who I supported, which was a strange position to be in.

On election day I went to the polling station, where drinks were freely distributed by contingents of both candidates, and cast my ballot, and awaited the results.

The next day, the most consternating surprise presented itself to Glory.

The vote was a tie.

184 votes for Martin Cadwell.

184 votes for Noah Spencer.

Unheard of! Incredible!

The town charter was consulted. In the event of a tie, it stated explicitly, a recount was in order. All the ballots had to be examined again, with witnesses from the camps of both candidates, and in public, so all could see.

I attended this recount. Several dozen of the town followed suit. We stood around a table, and watched while the town clerk took each ballot, displayed it to the audience, and then placed it in its appropriate pile.

The entire process, slow and painstaking, took more than a few minutes.

While the recount proceeded, I heard conversations around me. People were discussing the merits of democracy.

Such high-toned talk fell on my ears with a considerable dose of irony attached to them. If I had been presented to the world as my natural sex, that is, if people knew I was a woman, then I would not have been allowed to vote.

And yet, these men around me pontificated about the greatness of democracy and the purity of the vision of the founding fathers who saw to it that people were allowed to control their own destiny by means of the ballot.

I found myself more than a little angry. In fact, I found that I could not contain my anger.

"My dear sirs," I finally said, in the deep and gravelly voice I had adopted since my arrival, "one cannot speak of democracy until all citizens are granted suffrage. Even, if I may say, Natives, naturalized foreigners, and—" here I cleared my throat "—the fully half of the population known as women."

You would have been able, at that moment, to hear the sound of a cockroach skittering across the floor, such was the ensuing silence.

Then the assembled voters of Glory erupted in laughter.

"That's a good one, Robin," said one rancher.

"Yes," said another. "I'll go home and tell my wife that she must vote in the next election. For the sake of democracy and freedom."

More laughter.

I felt myself turning red. I was about to muster more arguments for my position when the clerk raised his voice above the laughter.

"The recount is completed," he said.

Silence fell on the room. We were all hushed.

"No change," said the clerk. "The result is still a tie."

"Then we shall have two sheriffs," said someone from the back.

"Impossible," said another in answer.

"Then what?" said a third rancher. "We are in a conundrum."

"More like a pickle," said someone else.

"The town charter is clear," said the clerk. He pulled out a ragged and wrinkled bit of paper and read from it.

"In the event the recount should result in a tie, the winner of the election shall be determined by the flip of a coin."

Upon these words, another eruption of noise from the crowd. "Ridiculous!" "Insane!" "Coins have no judgement."

The clerk quelled the noise with his hands once more.

"We must follow the charter," he said. He reached into his pocket and pulled out a quarter.

He held it up for the crowd to see, displaying one side, then the other, assuring us all that the coin was fair.

I was close enough to see that it was.

"This is how it shall go," said the clerk. "Mr. Cadwell. Mr. Spencer. Please step forward."

Martin Cadwell and Noah Spencer had been in the back of the room, keeping a respectful distance. They elbowed their way forward and stood in front of the clerk.

The clerk pointed to Cadwell. "When I toss the coin into the air," he said, "you shall call it. Heads or tails. You will state your preference while the coin is in the air and you will be as loud and clear as possible. Understood?"

Cadwell nodded and held up his fists and shook them in a little victory celebration, which was certainly premature, but that did not stop his supporters from roaring their approval.

"I will allow the coin to fall to the table. Then I will examine the coin and tell the result.

"Is this all understood?"

"We're letting God decide," said someone from the back.

Murmurs of assent followed the remark. Some in the room thought that God should not have a vote, me among them, but what could one do? The charter was clear, and if we did not do the coin flip, how would we decide?

"I think letting God decide the election is good enough for me," said Noah Spencer, then raised his own fists and imitated Cadwell's victory motions.

His supporters erupted, as Cadwell's had only a moment before.

The clerk waited for the noise to settle.

He licked his lips, adjusted his legs so his stance was a little wider. He made a fist, and presented it to the room so that his thumb was at the top, then he placed the coin on his thumb.

A hushed silence fell on the room. I could feel the heat of breaths all around me.

Just before the clerk was to launch the coin into the air, a hand clapped on my shoulder. I turned around to see the judge look me squarely in the face.

"Hold up," he said. "Stop these proceedings."

The clerk blinked.

Everyone looked at the judge.

"This *person* here," he said as he pointed to me, "will determine the results of this election."

My face drained of blood. I felt a trembling in my knees.

"Whatever do you mean?" I asked.

"Do not attempt to deceive me or the town any longer," said the judge. "It is my contention that you are not allowed to vote on the question of the sheriff."

"Indeed," I said, "and why is that?"

"On account of your sex."

I took in a deep breath. Everyone looked at me. I wished to escape but knew I could not.

"Do not deny it any longer," said the judge. "You are a woman.

Do not put us through the embarrassment of proving it to this group."

The clerk's mouth fell open. The two candidates looked at me with awe in their eyes.

"This is not so," I said.

"It is so," said the judge. Then he looked deep into my eyes.

Of course he knew the truth and could demonstrate it in a most unseemly way. I felt it was in him to do so.

I waited a few more beats before allowing that the judge was correct. I released my deep and gravelly voice to the ether and spoke in my natural tones. "You are correct," I said. "I am a woman."

"Ha," said the judge as he turned to the crowd. "Why this woman would pass herself off as a man is her own business, but the work of democracy is our business. Only male landowners are allowed to vote. And because of that, this woman's ballot is null and void. She should not have voted."

All in the room, including me, had to agree that that was the case. I knew it when I voted. I may have considered the provision unfair, but that did not change the fact that it was the law of the land.

"So now," said the judge, "the coin is not needed. All we need determine is who this woman voted for. Once that is settled, we can declare her vote for that candidate retracted and the other one shall be declared the winner and our new sheriff."

This met with approval from all present. I felt the heat of attention on me and it was not pleasant.

"So," said the judge. "My dear woman. Please tell us how you discharged your ill-gotten right. Tell us who you voted for."

I knew perfectly well who I voted for. But I also knew that if I told the judge, then the other candidate would be declared the winner, the candidate I did not choose.

I worked through the ramifications, on the spot, quickly. All I had to do to insure my candidate would be the winner was to declare that I had voted for the other one, the one I did not vote for.

But I also, on the spot, knew that others in the room would have the same thought process. They would see how I held the power in my hands.

"Hold up," said the clerk. "We cannot determine for certain if she will be telling the truth."

The judge glared at the clerk.

The clerk cowered.

"My job," said the judge, "is dealing with liars every day." He swung his hand around the room, his finger extended. "When any of you come before me, it is more than an even chance that you are lying."

Chuckles and nervous laughs from everyone present.

"So you see," he said, "I am in the best position to determine the truth of the matter."

He turned his attention to me. Again.

"I ask once more, dear lady. For which candidate did you cast your vote?"

I could not pull away from his eyes. He leaned close to me. I stepped back. I collided with the table, the one with all the ballots in neat piles.

I had a name on my lips. I was about to state it when someone stepped forward, holding a ballot in his hand. He raised it high for all to see.

"I hold Robin's ballot in my hand," he said.

"What?" said the judge.

"You can see the X," he said. "It is drawn in a feminine manner."

The judge spread his hands and raised his head to the heavens. "Lord," he said, "please spare me."

"It is as I say," said the man. "Look at the flourish of the mark. See how it flows over the page and out of the box."

The judge sighed and turned from me and took the ballot from the man. "You cannot be serious," he said.

"But I am," said the man.

Others pressed close to the judge. They wanted to see the ballot. He pushed them away.

"Allow me room," he roared. His face, by this time, was red.

He looked at the ballot for perhaps half a minute. I took the opportunity to edge toward the door.

But I would not escape. The judge turned to me and asked me straight out. "Is this your ballot?"

"Ballots are secret," I said.

"Not yours," he said evenly, "as yours was cast illegally."

"It should not have been," I said. "I am a landowner."

"But not a male. The law is clear."

"The law is a sham," I said.

This was not received well by his honor. He turned redder. His eyes popped. I thought, given other circumstances, his head might have blown off his neck, but nothing of that manner occurred, save in my imagination.

He held the ballot before my eyes, not inches away. I was supported from behind by some strangers, who kept me from falling over. It was a strange sort of support, as though they really wanted to help me.

"Now," he said, "for the last time. Is this your ballot? Who did you *illegally* vote for?"

I barely glanced at the piece of paper. It showed that whoever had placed that mark had voted for my candidate. Was the mark mine? I could not tell. Who could recognize their own X out of hundreds of Xs?

"I do not know," I said.

Here the judge lost all patience. He grabbed me by the shoulders and was determined, I believe, to shake me to my core.

But now, against all expectations, I must report that the good people of Glory did not abandon me to this wretch. No, in deference to the demands of good behavior and in marked opposition to my expectations, several of these burly ranchers took the judge from behind and pulled him away from me and dragged him to the floor.

The judge sputtered his protestations.

They were ignored.

Indeed, more than a few of the citizens of Glory saw fit at that time to spit on the judge. He folded himself up on the floor and whimpered.

The clerk banged his hands on the table.

"We will have none of that," he said.

He pointed to Cadwell and Spencer. "Help the judge," he said.

The two candidates hesitated.

"Go!" said the clerk.

Martin Cadwell bolted from the clerk and went to the judge and helped him up. Noah Spencer remained next to the clerk and sneered at Cadwell.

I noted this with more than a little interest.

The judge stood and shook off Cadwell, but he would not be pushed away. Cadwell spoke in soothing tones to the judge. He offered him some consoling words, then helped the judge out of the room amidst hoots and hollers from everyone else.

The judge, as I have indicated, was a wretch. I was glad to see him go.

I joined in with the catcalls. It felt most agreeable to taunt him in that way.

We clapped as the judge finally stumbled out the door, leaning on Martin Cadwell.

"Now then," said the clerk.

I turned to him.

"You seem to hold all the cards," he said. "Will you tell us who you voted for? Or will we resort to the coin?"

I stood there, amidst the landowners of Glory, and felt the power of my own decision. I could determine the future of Glory, at least for the next few years. I had only to state my preference, and the other candidate would be sheriff.

I took in deep breaths.

I looked squarely at Noah Spencer, who had chosen not to help the judge.

Everyone awaited my answer.

My hands trembled. Blood coursed through my veins rapidly,

it seemed, as though they needed to lift me up and hold me before the judgement of the universe.

"I came to Glory," I said to the room, "so that I might find some freedom of my own. I escaped an intolerable situation and went West to find a place where I might live without threat of harm.

"And now I find that I have more than freedom. I have something akin to power. At least for the moment."

The men stepped away from me. Out of respect or disgust, I could not say. Certainly some would accord me respect, but others would be appalled by such talk of freedom from a woman. We were not free. We were bound by custom and law to be something other than free.

"I state now," I said, "clearly and unequivocally, that I cast my illegal ballot for none other than this man who stands before you: Noah Spencer."

Mr. Spencer's eyes fell.

The room exploded in mixed cheers and protestations.

"By the power invested in me by the city of Glory," said the clerk, "I declare Martin Cadwell the new sheriff of this fair town."

Then he banged his hand on the table.

I ran from the hall and went down the street. I found the judge and Martin Cadwell shading themselves on a bench next to the general store.

They both looked at me.

"Congratulations," I said to Mr. Cadwell. "You are the new sheriff."

The judge and Cadwell looked surprised.

"You voted for Spencer?" asked Cadwell.

I looked at the judge, the one who was so sure he could tell a liar from a truth teller. He looked pathetic now, his clothes stained by the expectorations of his own townspeople.

He looked up at me, as though I could tell him truths he did not know. Or so I fancied.

"You are an abuser of power," I said.

He had no answer for me.

I turned to Cadwell. "No," I said. "I voted for you. But I told everyone I did not. So you could be sheriff."

He swallowed, hard, then rose and shook my hand.

"But why?"

"Because of what you did for him," I said, pointing to the judge.

"But you hate him," he said.

"I believe everyone deserves kindness," I said. "And so it appears to be your belief as well."

The judge looked shocked.

Cadwell blinked. "You will not regret it," he said.

I looked at him, then at the judge. They were both still men and would remain so. And I was still a woman and would remain so to the end of my days. I did not know if other things would change, but I was ready to hope for them.

"I look forward to many years of no regret," I said.

Royalty

THE KING'S ARMY had subdued the rebellion in which disgruntled peasants, objecting to the warlike actions of the monarch, had attempted to defeat the king and his army from a strategic vantage point in the countryside. Their campaign proved to be completely inadequate and their defeat was yet another victory in a long string of successes for the king. The royal tattooist was called in from the village to mark the occasion on the king's arm.

She arrived early in the morning, and was ushered into the king's chambers where the king and his ministers were conducting royal business. No one in the court was aware that the tattooist's people came from the very peasants that the king had just crushed. They knew her only as a simple poor woman, found one afternoon in the streets of the village, who had an amazing talent with needle and ink.

She bowed to the king, who barely noticed her. While she prepared her inks and needles, the king talked to his ministers. The tattooist had long ago learned to keep her ears from listening, but this time she could not help herself. The king and his ministers were designing a large prison to house the defeated peasants. Much better than executing them, said the king to his minister of labor, since we can use them for slaves.

Quite right, said the minister. Good thinking, your highness.

The tattooist bowed her head and awaited the king's order. The king, seeing her in such a suitably humble pose, rolled up his sleeve and rested his arm on his throne. A fine sword, he said to the tattooist. With good crisp detail. I want it to shine. Can you manage that?

The tattooist nodded and set to work. A sword would be easy. She was sure the king wanted it because that particular weapon, according to village gossip, had been the most used during the quelling of the recent conflict. Many peasants, some of them relatives of the tattooist, had been cut in half by swords wielded by the king's men on horseback.

The king watched the tattooist work for a few minutes, apparently fascinated by the needles, then turned back to his ministers. We'll need a high wall, said the king, to keep the slaves where we want them until we need to use them.

The ministers all nodded. We have taken that into account, they said. We can have the prison built within a few weeks.

The king's eyes brightened. Using slave labor, right? he said.

All the ministers laughed and nodded at his witticism. Quite so, your highness, they said, quite so.

The king leaned back. The sword was taking shape nicely on his arm as the tattooist, head bent to her task, dipped her needle in ink and pricked the king repeatedly. With each insertion of her needles, she wiped away excess ink and oozing blood with a cloth. She worked with great concentration, her entire being focused on her task. The king did not flinch at all with the pain, which the tattooist knew was not inconsiderable. She was also aware that upon the king's death, he had directed that his skin be removed from his body, the individual tattoos cut into frameable pieces and hung around the palace as works of art. Many in the court considered this a decidedly grisly project and a few even had the nerve to tell the king himself that such an undertaking was completely inappropriate. But the king would not listen to naysayers. He commanded his critics to be silent. They obeyed, as much for their own protection as to uphold respect for the king's authority.

What this meant for the tattooist was that her designs were destined to be treated as works of art. This simple fact made her want to do the best job she could.

She had already tattooed the king many times. He liked her designs and deemed them worthy of preservation.

The king drank great quantities of ale while the tattooist went about her work. The ministers refrained from joining the king in drinking. They wanted to keep their wits about them. They spoke of the need for garden space in the prison, so the peasants could feed themselves. They ironed out the legal status of any babies born in the prison. They would be citizens of the king's land and therefore subject to his rule, but would not enjoy the same legal status as babies born to non-slaves. The slaves would not be taxed, of course, as they would gain nothing from their labor. All their work would be at the service of the king. And so on. So many fine points of law and logistics to resolve.

Such considerations were tedious, but necessary, and no one in the room felt that maintaining these slaves would be anything but beneficial to the king and his kingdom.

The tattooist finished the sword and bowed her head. The king looked at her work and proclaimed his admiration for its artistry and accurate depiction. He asked his ministers to examine it.

They all looked closely and uttered words of praise. The king beamed. He sent the tattooist back to her lodging in the village.

Later that night, the village was in an uproar. The tattooist, asleep in her bed, awoke without surprise. She went outside where throngs filled the streets. The king is dead! they cried. The king is dead!

The tattooist had already disposed of the remaining poisonous ink by pouring it onto the ground as she left the king's palace. If the king's men came looking for her, they would find only her normal inks, completely safe and standard.

She was beyond reach on this matter. No one could trace the king's demise to her actions.

The tattooist returned to her room and went back to sleep.

The next day she was once again called to the palace. The queen, displaying an enormous amount of grief involving wails and the clutching of her own clothing in desperate spasms, directed the tattooist to cut her designs from the king's skin. The tattooist bowed her head and whispered her assent to the request. She was given an assistant to help with the task.

Tell me when you are finished, said the queen. I will need to bury the king then.

The tattooist nodded and went to the room where the king lay on a stone slab. Several guards stood against the walls of the room, watching the king and watching her. The tattooist was born a peasant and so had seen many animals skinned by her father and grandfather. She had learned to skin animals herself. Removing the king's hide from his flesh was no different.

She directed her assistant to prepare bowls of warm water. He did as he was told, as though the tattooist was royalty herself, demanding obedience. The tattooist saw immediately how even such a small bit of power as this made her feel strong and practically invincible. She cut out squares of the king's skin, carefully peeled them from his body, then gently washed them in the water. Some of the guards averted their eyes from her work. The tattooist noted this with interest. They did not want to see their leader cut into pieces. This was amazing to the tattooist, since the king was nothing now, just dead muscle and bone.

The king bore nine tattoos. The tattooist had harvested six of them when the queen came into the chamber.

Your majesty, said the tattooist to the queen, do you think it wise for you to witness any of this?

The queen tried to be strong, but mere seconds later her legs gave way under her and she collapsed to the floor. The guards broke from the chamber walls and tried to assist her.

The tattooist made no move toward the queen. This was her grief, nothing to do with the tattooist. She continued to labor over the king. With the help of her assistant, she laid out the pieces of the king's skin on a towel to dry. She worked at a brisk pace while guards waved smelling salts under the queen's nose. The tattooist, using her mind's eye and her considerable imagination, could already see her images in frames and hung on the palace walls.

The queen coughed and sputtered. She reached up, trying for something out of her field of vision.

My love, she said, obviously in a state of delirium, where have you gone?

The tattooist turned from the king's gallery and stepped toward the queen.

I can help, said the tattooist. Bare your arm. I'll give you his image to keep for all time.

The queen put her head in her hands and wept.

The tattooist knelt beside the queen and began rolling up the sleeve of her dress. The guards, astonished, did nothing to stop her. No one did anything to stop her art. The tattooist, though she detested the king and his warlike ways, made a commemorative portrait of the king on the queen's upper arm and spared no pains in making the picture as lifelike and noble as possible. Such a detestable lie, portraying the king as righteous and benign. But the tattooist did not flinch from her task. She worked quietly and steadily. The queen's skin was soft and white. A noble woman's skin, of course, sheltered from work and the sun. Such a pristine canvas for the tattooist's art, for the lie she put down with such attention to detail, such meticulous rendering of lifelike features. The queen, so it seemed to the tattooist, gained stamina as the portrait took shape. By the time the image was complete, the queen had regained all her strength and color. She no longer looked as though she wanted to die with her king. This was good, thought the tattooist. She did not want the queen to die.

When the portrait was complete, the queen went to look at the tattoos that had been harvested from her king. They were arranged on towels on a table. They told a story, of sorts. Each of the king's conquests of his many enemies had been commemorated on his skin. Each one now looked like a page from history. The queen read over the book of the king's life.

Here was an image of a wooden sword, marking the time he and his brother got into a fight when they were mere boys. The king, only a prince at the time, had won that fight by clubbing his brother smartly on the head several times. Next to it, an arrow, commemorating the duel he fought as a young man, over the hand of the queen. A rival to the queen's affections had challenged the king. The king, employing his considerable skills in archery, slew the rival. Next, a dagger, which the king had used to kill a would-be assassin early in his reign.

The king favored all kinds of weapons. His body had been a catalog of martial hardware.

The queen seemed to approve of the sight of these images laid out for her viewing. You have done an admirable job, she said to the tattooist. Not only in making the pictures in the first place, but in removing them from the king.

The tattooist bowed. Thank you, your majesty, she said.

Next to the dagger, another sword, taken from the king's back. This one was his first victory against the peasants. A war he had begun, and ended, swiftly, decisively. It was during this campaign that the tattooist first learned of the king and his ways. And the first time she determined that she would stop his destructive campaigns. She moved to the village and made it known that she had some talent as an illustrator of skin. The king heard of her prowess and, fond of tattoos himself, had her come to the palace and place images on his back, his legs, his chest. The tattooist did as she was commanded, building trust in her from the king and the court, until she got to the point where they chose not to search her as she entered the palace.

And so it was, on the day of the last tattoo, she made sure

that she brought poisonous inks for the king. To make an image of ultimate power for his farewell. That image was the sword, her finest work. It lay spread out on the towels at the end of the row, after more daggers, other swords, and bows and arrows. The king had led a full life of killing.

The room was still and alive with portent. All awaited the verdict of the queen. Would she approve of these pictures being hung in the palace? How could she? The very thought was repulsive.

So many victories, said the queen, and it all comes to this. Pieces of his skin to tell what he was, what he did. Her voice did not break or even quaver.

The tattooist remained silent with her head bowed. The guards glanced at her, as though looking for some guidance on the limits of their own behavior. How could this peasant woman, this wielder of ink and needles, bring solace to the grieving queen?

The queen directed the tattooist to make frames and properly display the tattoos from her king. The tattooist nodded her assent. Of course, she said.

The tattooist worked diligently for the rest of the day. With her assistant, she stretched the king's skin onto frames and tacked them down. She hung them all around the palace. She herself thought the enterprise had its grisly aspect, but she set aside such feelings. She was working for a higher purpose and the images— *her* images—did possess surprising beauty. Such beauty was not to be discounted.

When she finished she went to the queen to tell her the task was done. The queen nodded and walked about the palace, stopping at each picture while the tattooist walked behind her. At each stop, the queen kissed and stroked the king's skin, displaying disarming tenderness. The tattooist, seeing this, averted her eyes, unwilling to witness such odd intimacy.

When the queen completed her tour, she sighed and issued her first command as leader of her people and as supreme authority in the palace and the land.

She directed that the peasants be released back to the countryside and no measures be taken against them, their descendants, or their land. The tattooist heard the proclamation without betraying a single emotion. She bowed her head deeply, silently, and reverently.

Curse Island

IT WAS THE queen's wish that the rock known as Curse Island be destroyed.

The king, on the other hand, wished that Curse Island be more accessible.

My dear queen, he said, many of our subjects cannot get to Curse Island. We should make it safer so that everyone can shout their opinions to the heavens.

The heavens do not concern me, said the queen, it is the cursing that troubles my soul.

Curse Island was many miles from the palace. It was a mostly barren rock in the middle of an enormous lake with only some scrubby bushes growing on it and bits of moss here and there, like forgotten splotches of color on an artist's studio floor. The wind howled over Curse Island constantly and waves lashed the shore at all hours of the day and night.

There was no beach, for Curse Island was too crude to allow such an amenity. To get to it, hopeful cursers had to risk being smashed against the rocks. Every year several visitors to Curse Island came to just such an end.

The king had been there several times to witness for himself the allure of Curse Island. He saw nothing in the rock itself, but he did feel the freedom of the place. He understood why his subjects would put their lives in jeopardy to reach it.

When he was on Curse Island, he was able to express his annoyance and anger with his subjects.

He climbed up to the center of it, barely 500 feet from the water. He stood and felt the wind howl over him. He lifted his mouth high and let loose with the most vile and colorful invectives against his lazy subjects.

He told the sky, in no uncertain terms, that the peasants were always begging for food and shelter and they hated paying their fair share of taxes, as though the king owed them a living.

He especially offered his opinion that not a single one of them had the brains of a flea. They were stupid and worshipped a stupid god and if they all died tomorrow it would not be too soon.

Such outbursts were contrary to the king's usual nature. When subjects came to court to ask for his assistance and wisdom, he was, at least outwardly, completely benign and generous. He listened carefully and passed judgement with mercy and restraint.

Inside, of course, he had no patience for any of it. He wanted only to ride and hunt, eat and drink, gamble and fight, and cavort with the queen. All of these things he did, but not as much as he would have wished since so much of his time was taken with his subjects and their incessant *needs*.

When he returned from Curse Island, the queen remarked that he seemed like a completely new man.

I am, dear queen, he said. I have found the secret of happiness: Curse Island.

She scowled at the suggestion. There is no such thing as a secret of happiness, she said. And Curse Island is a menace. Do you know that the subjects go there and describe us in the most profane terms?

I do, indeed, said the king. It is most wonderful.

I do not understand you, said the queen. They utter profanities directed at *us*. You and me.

That is what makes it wonderful, said the king. They let out their frustrations and return from Curse Island with renewed respect for life.

Ha! said the queen. What they do there is foment dissent and rebellion. Without us they would all surely perish.

Do not be so hard on them, said the king. They don't know any better. Peasants they were born and peasants they will die. Curse Island gives them a little bit of power, for a brief time.

The queen tried to convince the king that he was misguided at best, perhaps delusional at worst. But the king would not hear of it.

He ordered a regular ferry to Curse Island, assigning a sturdy ship to the route so that his subjects did not have to attempt a landing on Curse Island in their crude rafts. He posted guards at the rock around the clock, so that his subjects might feel safe and secure.

The king saw to it that the guards were deaf, so there was no possibility that they might return to the palace with tales of what certain peasants said on Curse Island. It was the king's conviction that the cursers needed complete freedom and that meant complete anonymity.

He commanded his engineers to carve a secure dock in the rock, sheltered and tame, that the ferry might moor securely and his subjects would not have to concern themselves with stepping off a pitching boat.

The queen, meanwhile, turned to her own resources. She went up to the top of the palace, where spires reached for the skies, and opened a window and put her hand through the opening to the outside air.

Her palm held seeds and presently several mooripah birds came to take the seeds. They perched on her fingers, tiny things with iridescent feathers and red eyes. As they took up the seeds with rapid dips of their heads, the queen raised her hand and whispered in their ears.

She told them all kinds of seeds would be theirs if they would simply fly to Curse Island, listen to what was said, and return with accurate reports of the complaints of the peasants.

The mooripah birds twitched their feathers as they ate and chirped into the air.

The queen listened to their staccato peeps and knew that she and the birds had an agreement.

ONCE THE KING had made Curse Island even more attractive than it had been, the peasants flocked to it with renewed vigor. Outings to Curse Island became a family affair, with parents, children, grandparents, and cousins all boarding the ferry and taking the ride there.

Most visitors had a routine from which they seldom varied. They would step off the docked ferry and without any fanfare or, indeed, any obvious preparations at all, walk up the rock face of the island.

Mooripah birds swirled around them, flocks of them, like a shining cloud. The peasants didn't care about the birds. They only wanted to reach the pinnacle of the island.

Once they did, with their hands clutching their garments closed and holding down their hats against the wind, they proceeded to curse the king and the queen.

He was a fat slob. She was a lazy slob. The king cared only for himself and his queen. The queen, even worse, cared only for herself. They, the king and queen, should be tossed from their thrones and given to the pigs to eat. Their corpses should be worm food, if worms could be found so lacking in self respect that they would foul themselves on the putrid royal flesh. Ha!

So liberating to say such things out loud. The wind took their words and carried them up and up and away.

The guards would watch over the peasants with some amusement. They had no idea what was being uttered, but they could see that the peasants said what they said with great gusto, as though they were bellowing their joy to the world.

One peasant in particular, a young man with long hair and scraggly beard, rode the ferry to the island every day. He stood at the pinnacle of Curse Island and spoke to the heavens at great length.

He was an orator, obviously. He used his hands as he spoke, waving them through the air as though he was swimming. The young man would come in any weather. It could be snowing and he would board the ferry and come. It could be raining a drenching, cold, and awful rain, and it would not stop the young man. He was dedicated to his ritual.

The mooripah birds flew through his words and took them into their ears and imprinted them on their brains and throats. They returned to the palace where the queen sat near the window at the topmost spire.

They flocked around her. The queen had ordered several feeders, filled with seed, be mounted around the room. The Mooripah birds came to the feeders and ate their fill, all the while chirping and tweeting and twittering and chortling.

The queen, conversant in the language of birds, took it all in. She turned red-faced with rage as she listened to their wish to see her killed.

Worse, she heard reports that some peasants wanted her dragged through the streets that all her subjects might spit on her.

Such reports filled the queen with sadness and even more anger at her husband. The king must not allow their subjects free reign to dredge up the most vile thoughts they had against the royal couple.

She told the king of what she heard.

And how have you heard these things? he asked. Did you go to Curse Island?

The mooripah birds told me, she said.

The king laughed. No, he said. That is not possible. You do not know the language of the mooripah.

I do, dear king, I do. And I listen and I tremble at the possibilities. The peasants are in revolt.

Nonsense, my dear, said the king. They are simply availing themselves of the opportunity to release resentments. It is a wonderful thing. Do you not see how they are now more docile and pleasant?

The queen, despite her hatred of Curse Island, had to agree with the king. The ones who came to the palace now were much more calm and solicitous than they had been before the improvements to Curse Island were made.

It is a false peace, said the queen. You will see. This is a nasty business.

He patted her hand. Do not worry yourself. Look at the results. That is all that matters.

I only hope that you are correct, said the queen, but I fear that you are not.

THE KING, SATISFIED that Curse Island had made his subjects happy and content, decided to take a hunting trip in the western woods. He assembled his party, bid farewell to the queen, and told her he would return in a week.

I will bring back venison, duck, goose, and more, he said. It will be a most bounteous expedition. You will want to be my queen as never before!

The queen bid him farewell and told him to be careful.

As she watched the hunting party disappear over the horizon, she ordered guards to bring the young man who so loved Curse Island for an audience with the queen.

He was dragged into the throne room a scant hour later. She let him stew in his fear for a further half hour before she entered the room and sat on the throne above him.

Your name, please, she said.

The young man, who should have been frightened by the possibility that he might be killed at any instant, displayed no hint of fear, or, indeed, any discomfort whatsoever. He stood tall and held his chin high. So unlike any peasant the queen had known. He was quite handsome. The queen was not immune to his charms, and her heart softened slightly. She knew she would not execute him this day.

Call me Stewart, he said.

A guard poked him in the side, hard, with the end of a staff. He doubled over.

Call me Stewart, your *majesty*, he said.

And why should I do that? asked the queen. Is that your name?

Yes, he said. Your majesty.

The queen breathed slowly three or four times. This one was strong and defiant. He could be the leader of a rebellion. She could see it in his eyes and his demeanor.

Do you hate me? asked the queen.

I don't know you, your majesty. I hate only your position.

My position?

Your power over your people is without consent of your people. You are a tyrant.

A tyrant? Indeed?

It is not your fault, said Stewart. Such is the nature of your place in society that you could not be anything less than a tyrant. I do not blame you.

And yet you curse me. Every day. On Curse Island. You say I insult the gods by living. You say I should beg the peasants for my bread. You say the king and I roast babies and eat them for our dinner. You say all these things.

Stewart's eyes darted from side to side. He knew the guards were deaf. How, then, did the queen know what he said on Curse Island?

It appears your majesty has powers unknown to me, said Stewart. I confess, I have said all these things.

And more, said the queen.

And more, said Stewart.

The guard raised his staff, but the queen put up her hand. Never mind, she said. Let him speak as he wishes. He clearly does not want to refer to me as his majesty.

Stewart met her eyes and looked as though he was going to nod, but did not. He only took in shallow breaths, as though he might breathe in poison if he inhaled deeply.

The queen studied Stewart. Why is that? she asked him.

No one should have the ability to grant life and death based on an accident of birth. The people should be able to govern themselves.

Indeed? said the queen. And have you not noticed that the people have nothing? Without royal largesse, you would surely all perish.

Only because you hold all the riches of the land. If it were made freely available to all, there would be no need of the wretched royal couple or your so called generosity.

It was as the queen had feared. Stewart was not an innocent releasing frustrations. He was a radical, bent on overthrowing the king and the queen.

She ordered him to be placed in a secure cell in the basement of the palace.

For how long, your majesty? asked Stewart. How long will you hold me against my will?

As long as I wish, she said. That is the power my blood has granted me.

Stewart cursed the queen and the king and the palace as guards dragged him away. The queen listened to his words as they echoed through the halls. She closed her eyes and whispered her own oaths.

Death to insolent peasants, she thought. Death to them all.

THE KING RETURNED bearing game exactly as he had predicted. He and his hunting party had done well. The queen met him at the palace gates and they embraced. This inflamed their passions and they repaired to the queen's chambers where they spent an energetic few hours.

While they were thus engaged, the palace staff saw that the larders were filled with fowl and game. Teams of cooks cured the meat and dried it and stored it for the months ahead.

The king was filled with delight and energy. Nothing like a successful hunting expedition to get his blood racing and make him see the world anew.

As they lay on the queen's bed, both of them sated and happy, the king turned to the queen. I think, he said, I shall repair to Curse Island. Will you accompany me?

I think not, my dear king.

Please, said the king. Just once. You cannot hate what you do not know.

But I do know, my king. I know it only too well.

I have a private boat, said the king. We will not have to mix with the peasants, you and I. We will be free to do as we wish.

The queen sighed. And you wish to curse the heavens?

The king roared with laughter. Not the heavens, my dear queen. You still do not see the power of the place. It is to curse life! All the life around us. It is to liberate our most horrible thoughts. Please come with me. I believe it will do you so much good.

The queen did not tell the king of Stewart, marinading in a damp and rat-infested cell at the bottom of the palace. She did not explain to him that Stewart expressed much more than simple irritation at the royal couple. She did not tell him that Stewart, an ambitious young man, wanted nothing more than to take away power from the royal couple.

Instead, she told the king that, once, just this once, she would go to Curse Island and see what all the fuss was about.

The king jumped as high as his bulk would allow, which was not excessive, but which, nevertheless, expressed to the queen his joy and love for life, the palace, their land, and her.

The queen, despite herself, smiled at him, her ridiculous love. The reason for her life.

THE KING AND queen eschewed a crew on their expedition to Curse Island. The king, as a boy, had once navigated water craft and still fancied himself skillful at the task.

He was not exactly that, not anymore, but he managed to get the ferry into the dock with not too much in the way of mishaps. A few bangs and dings here and there against the rocks, but nothing threatening a capsizing or other disaster.

He stepped off the ferry and turned back and extended a hand to his queen. She took it, raised her skirts, and placed her foot on the rock.

Immediately as she did so, a shock of energy shot through her body. It was as though the rock was possessed and passed on its spirit, through the queen's foot, and up her body to her head.

She wobbled. Her knee buckled. The king stepped forward, quickly and gallantly, to keep her from falling. She grabbed his shoulders to right herself.

Are you all right, my dear queen? asked the king with concern etched on his face.

She took a deep breath and righted herself and planted both feet on the rock. When she was sure she would not swoon or fall, she nodded.

I am, dear king, she said.

Very good, said the king. Let us climb, now.

They held hands as they walked. The queen stepped over fissures in the black material at her feet. She noted the rock was not nearly as barren as she had imagined it. There were shrubs here and there. Even small creatures, lizard-like things, that darted before them.

I did not know there was life on this rock, she said.

There was not for a long time, said the king. But after I began the ferry route, things changed. It is transforming. You see the shoots here and there? He pointed to small green plants, just beginning to sprout in the dirt that had collected in dips and valleys in the rocks.

Mooripah birds swirled around them. They did not chirp or twitter. They were there to collect sounds, not make them.

There are also many splashes of Mooripah bird droppings, said the king. You see?

The queen did see. White streaks everywhere. Tiny, but unmistakable, dotted Curse Island.

They are your friends, these mooripah birds, yes? asked the king.

I like them, said the queen. They are beautiful.

The king nodded. He kept walking. This way, he said.

As they rose the wind began to blow harder. It dragged across the queen's clothes which snapped the air in answer.

So windy, she said.

All the better to disperse the curses, he said. It is the glory of Curse Island. Whatever you say does not stay. It scatters to the four corners and makes the words lose their power.

An interesting theory, said the queen.

I think it a fact, said the king, not theory.

They continued without words, but not in silence. The wind whistled and hummed and howled and roared. So many permutations of air moving through air. The queen was quite flummoxed, not knowing if she should stand up against the forces or huddle herself down for protection.

When they arrived at the pinnacle of Curse Island, the king and queen released their hands. The queen leaned into the wind. It held her up. She fancied she could let herself fall and the wind would keep her from hitting the rock.

When do we start? she asked.

Any time, said the king. Let your spirit move you to words. Release the words and they will release you.

The queen raised her head high, conscious of its regal angle and conscious, too, that Stewart held his head in just exactly the same manner. She was ready to curse the very name Stewart, let alone the person who wore it.

After all, his name was not something he earned. It was blood given, was it not? Exactly as her power was blood given. More worthy than the whims of peasants. Blood was ancient and wise. So she had been taught.

She opened her mouth and told the wind, the air, the sky, the very ground and water around her, that the king was a pile of cow dung.

Further, she informed creation that he would lose a battle of wits with a rock. Any rock.

She did not stop. She went on to state that the king's grooming habits left her with a vile taste in her mouth, particularly his practice of trimming his toenails while on the throne.

Then there were his decisions as leader of the land. Was it truly necessary to set aside *so many acres* for a hunting preserve? How much room did it take to shoot an arrow into a dear's neck?

And so on. The queen continued for some time, how long, the king wasn't sure, but it felt like an eternity.

When she was finished, she felt buoyed up with an elated spirit, as though the very heavens itself had taken the time and opportunity to make her the happiest being anywhere.

She turned to the king. Her face was flush with excitement. She embraced him and he, reluctantly at first, then with slightly more enthusiasm, put his arms around her.

You were so right, said the queen. Curse Island is a blessing. I feel so free, as though all my burdens have been lifted.

That is well and good, dear queen, said the king. But there was hardly any conviction behind his words.

The queen sensed this immediately. She pulled back from him and looked into his eyes.

You didn't like what I said, she said.

No, he said.

But you wanted me to come here. You insisted.

I know.

And now you are upset because I went along with your suggestion.

Indeed, it is so, said the king. I never dreamed you had so many complaints about me. I expected you to say things about the peasants.

I meant to, but the spirit, as you said it would, moved me elsewhere.

The king nodded. I would have expected so much less, he said. Maybe that I snored. He shrugged.

No, said the queen. You will not do this. You will not bring me here then make me feel as though I have transgressed our trust because I did what you asked of me.

Let us go back to the palace, said the king.

No! said the queen. Your turn.

My turn?

She spun him around and pushed him toward the summit of Curse Island.

The entire land, including me, has cursed you. Now it's your turn. Curse me.

The king felt the wind around him. It attempted to tear off his jacket. He attempted to quell his rising rage, but there was no use. Curse Island pulled it from him.

The queen, he said to the wind, dresses frumpily and without concern for her appearance. She wears her hair in a manner befitting a peasant, not a monarch.

The queen stood to his side and applauded his efforts. Very good, she said with genuine encouragement. Do go on.

The queen is useless. She can do nothing. She needs servants to help her pee in a pot!

Excellent! said the queen, applauding. Continue, please.

The king did continue. He took up the question of the queen's lineage, making it clear that he did not care for her parents, or, indeed, any of her relatives. He questioned not only her intelligence, but her very sanity.

When he was finished, the wind still howled, but there was an air of sorrow about it. It was as though they had violated something.

The king had lost his joy. His shoulders slumped and his head hung low.

Curse Island has leveled us, dear king, said the queen.

Indeed, said the king. We have torn each other down until we are little more than lumps on the ground.

They stood next to each other, unable, or, indeed, unwilling, to step off the rock.

The others who come here, said the king, they don't curse their own.

Indeed, said the queen. They curse you and me, who are not their family.

Perhaps, said the king, we have made a misstep here today. It is not good that husband and wife should present such thoughts to the heavens.

I fear you may be correct, said the queen.

They descended to the harbor and their craft and returned to the palace. Later that day they presided over peasant disputes, as they always did. The king dredged up all the mercy and sympathy he could. The queen, for her part, tried to quell her impulse to punish the peasants. They all deserved it, of course, but she was conscious of the king's criticism of her.

They were an uneasy pair on their thrones. They wished only to get out of their responsibilities and repair to separate chambers where they might lick their wounds and hope that a good night's sleep would demolish the wall that had somehow grown up between them.

STEWART, MEANWHILE, HAD found allies among the guards who kept him in the cell in the basement of the palace. He never stopped speaking of the injustice of the monarchy and how the peasants needed to revolt against the king and the queen.

At first the guards would not tolerate his views. They beat him terribly. He sustained numerous cuts and bruises, but his spirit was not bruised in the least. As long as he had lips, tongue, and teeth, he continued.

Eventually some of the guards began to take in his words. They found he made a great deal of sense. Why *should* the king and queen have power over the land and its peoples, simply because they were born from a line that took the land, by force, many hundreds of years ago from another family?

The guards began murmuring amongst themselves. They knew the royal couple had riches hidden away in a remote part of the land. Gold, silver, and jewels. No one knew exactly where these riches were, but all knew it represented the worth of the kingdom. Why weren't these riches made accessible to the masses?

Why indeed?

They asked Stewart if he knew where they were.

He said he did not, but that even if he did he would not take them for himself. It was his hope to turn the peasants against the royal couple and, as a group, find the wealth and use it to make a better life for everyone.

This was very attractive to the guards, who decided they would see what interest there was among the rest of the palace workers.

Quite aware that what they were doing could be grounds for execution, they boldly approached maids and cooks, stone layers and stable keepers. Indeed, within a few days they had recruited much of the palace against the king.

Curse Island had primed them for revolt. All they needed was a guiding spirit, a leader who might be bold enough to defy the royal couple.

The guards told Stewart that they were with him.

We will follow you to the riches of the land, they said, and we will insure that wealth is distributed evenly.

Stewart, still nursing his wounds and a grudge against the guards, brightened and held up his hands.

Comrades! he said. We will take the palace in solidarity!

The guards roared their approval and lifted Stewart up on their shoulders and carried him from the lower levels of the palace, up and up to the throne room. They deposited him on the king's throne and cheered him.

Stewart liked the feel of the fine leather on his back and bottom.

He could get used to this luxury.

THE KING, IN his chambers, heard the commotion from below. He jumped out of bed and went to the door and opened it. He was met by three of his guards who pushed him back.

What is this? said the king.

A revolution, said one of the guards.

The king, unwilling to believe what his own eyes were seeing, pressed forward, as though he could get through the guards.

One of them struck him in the face with a rod. The king reeled back and fell. His only thoughts were of the queen.

Where is my wife, he said. Where is my dear queen? What have you done to her?

Nothing, said one of the guards.

I demand you bring her to me, said the king.

On the word *demand* one of the guards stepped forward and bent down low so his mouth was close to the king's ear.

No more demands, your former majesty, said the guard. From now on you may *request* or *beg*, but your demanding days are over.

The king, sensing the momentous change in his circumstances, did not lament his fate or curse the heavens. He was a pragmatic man and a shrewd king, when he had to be.

Very well, he said. He put up his hand.

The guard struck it with his rod. The king pulled his hand back. It was bruised and possibly broken.

I need no more proof of your mastery over me, he said. May I be permitted the luxury of a visit with my queen?

The guards stood around him, unsure, on some level what to do next. They had taken the palace, it was true, but once one *has* the palace, what does one do next? There were no guidelines for their present situation.

We will bring her, said a guard.

And so they did. A few minutes later they led the queen to the king's chamber. They were very polite and did not unduly pressure the queen with pushes or shoves.

The queen, for her part, chose not to defy the guards. She, too, had discerned the situation quickly and determined that her best chance for survival was compliance, at least for now.

The queen and king fell upon each other as soon as they were within close proximity. They embraced with strength and power. They both wept and uttered apologies.

The first chance I get, said the king, I will destroy Curse Island. Destroy it.

Oh, my dear king, said the queen. You are hurt. She put her

hand on his wounds. The king flinched. The queen drew back blood. I fear it is too late for that, she said. We have sown much that cannot be unsown. I fear they wish to kill us and lack only the conviction to do so. But that will come soon enough.

The king noted that the queen chose to include herself in the debacle that was Curse Island. He felt a swelling in his heart, knowing she was still his ally.

Presently they released each other from their embraces. Some of the guards looked away from the royal couple, embarrassed by being in such close proximity to the intimate murmurings of a couple in love.

Others, less prone to sentiment, snickered at them.

Revel in your love, said one of them. It's all you have now.

Then the guards left the chamber and closed the door behind them.

Do you know anything of this rebellion? asked the king.

Nothing, said the queen. I discovered a troublemaker among the peasantry. A rabble rouser. I had him tossed into the dungeon.

Indeed? said the king. You did not tell me.

I feared you would put him to death.

You thought *I* would put him to death? That is more your method, is it not?

What you say, dear king, is so, but I did not want blood on my hands while you were gone. It is a lonely business to execute someone. I needed you near me if I would take such an action.

I see, said the king.

Also, said the queen.

Yes? said the king.

He is a young man, and very beautiful. It seemed wrong to destroy such beauty. I was blinded to his evil and could not kill him.

The king nodded. Alas, he said, it is too late for that now. We must escape the palace and find a way to the royal treasure. With it we can find a new land and begin a new life. Are you with me?

The queen raised her hand high and the king grasped it in his meaty hands, then lifted her up.

The treasure, he said, is four miles distant, to the east, in the center of the game preserve, under a cluster of seven oaks.

As he spoke, mooripah birds swirled around him. They had entered through an open window in the king's chambers, in search of seed.

They did not chirp or tweet. The only sound was the humming of their tiny wings.

ONE OF THE guards told Stewart that he daily took seed to bird feeders at the top of the palace.

Indeed? said Stewart.

The king and queen like birds, said the guard. One kind in particular. The mooripah bird.

I know this bird, said Stewart. We have them where I live.

They talk to the queen, said the guard.

This is a great skill the queen possesses, said Stewart. But it is not unique. I, too, have this skill.

Then you must listen to the mooripah birds, said the guards. They have tales to tell.

Stewart agreed. He went up to the top most spire of the palace, where the queen's bird feeders stood. Stewart and the guard filled all the feeders with seed.

Then they sat and waited.

Within minutes mooripah birds, flocks of them, entered the room and began taking up seed in their beaks. As they did so, they emitted numerous chirps and tweets. Stewart listened carefully. His expression went from puzzlement to enlightenment within a few minutes.

I have learned something from the birds, he said.

Yes? said the guard, what is it?

They have listened to the conversation of the king and queen.

Yes? said the guard.

I now know that Curse Island must be destroyed.

The guard's eyebrows rose on his face. Curse Island destroyed?

Yes, indeed, said Stewart. The king and queen wish to make Curse Island their home.

But no one can live there, said the guard.

Nevertheless, we must see to it that it is broken into pieces. Many pieces.

The guard scratched his head. Comrade Stewart, he said, this is most strange, what you are telling me. Who cares about Curse Island anymore? We must find the royal treasure.

And we will, said Stewart. We will. Until then, we must do what the heavens ask of us.

The guard shrugged his shoulders. Stewart had the skill and will to overthrow the royal couple. Perhaps he knew what he was doing. No one else did.

Here's what you do, said Stewart. Find every able-bodied person in the land. Equip them with breaking and cutting tools. Swarm over Curse Island and tear it to pieces and cast the pieces into the lake that they might drown their power. Do you understand? Say it is on orders of me, Stewart.

The guard did as he was asked. Within hours, an expedition of hundreds of peasants sailed to Curse Island and set upon it.

Stewart wasted no time. He found several sturdy bags and draped them over his shoulder. He set out for the spot the mooripah birds described.

He did not forget to bring a shovel.

THE KING AND queen waited for darkness, then tore up bed linens into strips and tied them together.

The queen had her doubts that they would hold the king, but she did not express them. She was sure the king had similar doubts. If they went out the window and their makeshift rope gave way, then they would smash on the rocks below and that would be the end of them. Better such an end to their lives than to be held prisoner in their own palace.

They pushed the king's bed closer to the window and tied the end of the sheet rope to the post, as an anchor.

The queen went down first. She used the knots as footholds and grasped the rope around her hands. All went well. She got to the bottom and stepped off the rope and stood, in the dark, on the rocks.

She called up to the king. Your turn, she said.

The king moved his bulk through the window and held onto the rope.

But his grasp was weak from the wound he sustained earlier. His hands slipped from the rope. He fell and began to tumble. He reached for a hold onto something, but there was only air and it would not, could not, hold him up.

The queen, standing below him, saw a great shadow in the night hurtling toward her. She stepped aside and screamed.

The king slammed against the rocks.

The sound of broken bones splintered the air. The king released his last breath moments later, before he and the queen could bid each other farewell.

AS DAYLIGHT BROKE, the land found Stewart on a swift horse, bound for the center of the hunting grounds.

He was not skilled in riding a horse, as his family had been too poor to own one, but he managed as best he could. He came close to falling only once, and righted himself by grabbing his horse's mane.

As the sun rose above the horizon, Stewart slowed his horse and looked around. Fog rose up from the grass. It obscured his view. The air was cold and fresh, as though it had been pulled from some northern region and dropped here in front of him.

His hands and feet stung from cold. Puffs of steam jetted from his horse's nostrils.

He saw the grouping of oaks, as it had been described to him by the mooripah birds.

He slipped down from his steed and pulled a shovel from his

pack and approached the trees. He circled them, thinking where someone might bury a treasure.

No intuition guided him, but presently he found a bit of ground that looked like it had been worked. The grass on top of it was of a different color and texture than the rest.

He fell to his knees and plunged his shovel into the dirt and pulled up a clump of it and tossed it aside.

The soil was soft here. He was sure he had the correct location.

He spent the next hour digging feverishly. Sweat poured from his face. His arms grew sore and tired. His legs began to wobble from the effort. He had gone down perhaps five feet when his shovel blade struck something hard.

He dropped the shovel and bent down and pushed aside dirt. Under the dirt he found a wooden chest.

His heart filled up with wonder and joy.

He raised the lid of the chest and reached his hand down into the interior.

He touched coins. There was little light there, but he was sure they were gold. He touched stones. Surely priceless jewels. He called his joy to the heavens. Instead of cursing the royal couple, the thanked them for putting this treasure where he could find it. And he did not forget to say a prayer to the mooripah birds.

He filled his pouches with the booty from the chest and tossed them up to the surface, one at a time. It took him a long while, but he was able to fill several bags and by the time he was finished, the chest was empty.

He climbed up and out of the hole he had dug, feeling like he had accomplished the most important task of his life.

He stood up and raised his arms to the heavens.

At precisely that moment, the queen, who had been hiding behind one of the seven trees, advanced on Stewart and struck him in the head with a thick limb.

Stewart went down immediately. He put his hands to his head and screamed. He looked up at the sky. The face of the queen looked down at him.

You thought to steal from me? she said.

You stole, said Stewart. You did not earn any of this.

Neither did you, she said, but you are here, alone, without any of your revolutionary comrades. Were you thinking to take all this back to the palace?

Stewart, seeing that the queen had discerned his plans, did not try to deceive her.

We can take the treasure, he said. You and I.

You forget the king, said the queen.

The king, said Stewart. You don't need the king. He's a fat slob.

He's also dead, said the queen.

Stewart looked confused, as though the queen had told him he had wings and could fly.

Dead?

Trying to escape, said the queen.

All the better, then, said Stewart. He's out of the way. Now you and I can take these riches and—

He did not finish. The queen, while Stewart spoke, had bent down and retrieved Stewart's shovel. She raised it high and brought it down, repeatedly, on Stewart's skull.

CURSE ISLAND DID not stand a chance against the onslaught of the peasantry of the land. They took to its destruction with gusto and an admirable sense of duty, indeed, of responsibility.

The queen, still wearing clothes streaked with mud and dirt from having pushed the treasure back into the hole, and with streaks of Stewart's blood mixed in, approached the remains of the island on a crude raft.

When she got close, the guards saw her and mistook her for a peasant. They threw her a rope and hauled her in.

One of the guards took her hand. She stepped onto a landscape of rubble and dust. The wind did not howl.

Welcome, comrade, said the guard.

Thank you, said the queen.

The guard, suddenly realizing who he was talking to, froze. Your majesty? he said.

The queen lifted her head so that her chin rose high. She gulped in great lungfuls of air. She wanted to curse them all, every one of them, but she found she didn't have the breath to do so.

Not anymore, she said.

Weedhead

OWLSPEAK WAS NOT used to living in a wooden shack, and this one, with its tiny windows and moldy corners, did nothing to endear her to the idea. The worst thing about it was the ceiling: it hid the sky, a fact that caused her much consternation. How could anyone live without the sparkling sky above them, looking down with grace and beauty?

Owlspeak never thought she would have to hide herself away, but her age had caught up with her, not to mention her infirmity, and now, reluctantly, she insulated herself against the wild world with walls and a roof. She could no longer spend the time outdoors that she did decades ago, or even a few years ago. Her bones were always chilled and she constantly needed blankets wrapped around her. Even in this relatively mild time of the year, when apples still clung to their trees, before the snows of winter descended on her land, she found her teeth chattering in the early morning hours from the cold and she resented the dying embers in the stove, useless after spending their heat during the night. She wanted to be like those embers: dead and gone from the world. What a relief that would be.

And now what was this? A rattling at her front door to further disturb her rapidly waning sleep. She rose reluctantly from her bed, shivering the whole time, wrapped a blanket around her ample form and her fat legs, waddled to the door, and pulled it open.

A young woman—surely no older than sixteen summers—stood in front of her.

"What's this?" said Owlspeak. "Who are you?"

"Hera," said the young woman. She lowered her head. "My name is Ravenspring. I seek your gift." Her too-long rusty hair, entwined with weeds and covered with burrs, fell from her shoulders and draped itself across the handle of her sword, which she held with the requisite reverence accorded any fine weapon by its owner. The point of the blade was embedded in the ground, as was proper when approaching one's elder. However, Owlspeak's practiced eye saw that the weapon was not a fine one at all. Its workmanship was inferior, especially in the curve of the blade and the sharpness of its edge. She felt sure that if she hefted it, it would have no temperament of its own. Instead it would attempt to usurp the power of a more accomplished sword. This did not immediately disqualify the girl from serious consideration, but it did bespeak a certain lassitude in her practice. Or merely a life without access to some of the finer objects of a warrior's arsenal.

"And what is your name or your quest to me?" said Owlspeak.

Ravenspring did not look up. "Hera, there are whispers in the land. You will pass soon and need someone to carry your gift. I wish to be that person."

Owlspeak scowled. She wanted to smack this upstart across the head and send her sprawling to the ground. She could do it, too, even in her enfeebled dotage. However, she did approve of the seeker's demeanor: brazenness touched with a dash of humility. Owlspeak debated whether to close the door on her or let her in.

She regarded the girl for several seconds, then stepped to one side. "Come in Weedhead," she said.

To her credit, the girl did not flinch or protest at her new name. She lifted her head, pulled her sword from the ground, and walked past Owlspeak into her house.

"Have you traveled far?" said Owlspeak. "Are you hungry?"

"I come from Gilderdale," said Ravenspring. "A tiny village to the east."

"I know it," said Owlspeak. "Three or four days journey from here. Wheat growers and sheep herders, mostly. A soft people. I had a man from there once. Years ago. But he disappointed me and I threw him to the wolves."

"I assure you," said Ravenspring, "that I am not soft."

Owlspeak took in her ragged clothing made of torn leather, probably sheepskin. Her shoes had seen better days: they looked as though they had been scuffed over rocks and gravel. Surely there were rips in the sole, by the look of the sides. The girl was no flower: she had muscular arms and her legs looked as though she could run at a good clip. She held herself awkwardly, as though she was not comfortable in Owlspeak's house, indeed, in Owlspeak's presence.

"How do I look to you?" said Owlspeak. "Do I disappoint you?"

"Your heroic deeds are known to all," said Ravenspring. "You could never disappoint anyone."

It was true that Owlspeak, with her ability to understand animal language, was able to thwart an invasion of the land years ago, but that was long in the past. She used to ride into battle with the best fighters, their complete equal, and hold her own, killing many of the enemy. Her blood coursed fast and hot then, but her sword swinging days were over now. Time for the next generation to step up. The land always needed protecting. Was this woman—this *girl*—the one to take over from her now?

She reached out and grabbed the girl by her hair and pulled her close. The girl moved her arms to resist at first, then relaxed and let Owlspeak grip her locks. Owlspeak knew that her breath was awful and her sweat had long turned rancid. These were unfortunate consequences of her ailment and her indifference, now, to making herself presentable to society. What society? She was alone in her shack, waiting for death.

She watched for some twitch in Weedhead's nose, some indication of revulsion. None came. Then she pulled a knife from out of the holder strapped to her thigh and put its blade to the roots of Weedhead's hair. Most girls her age would sooner die than lose their hair. Owlspeak jerked the blade. A sheaf of Weedhead's hair tumbled to the floor along with burrs and dried leaves.

"What did you kill on your journey here?" said Owlspeak.

"Rabbits for my dinners," said Weedhead. "Wolves in self defense. And bears for sport."

"Sport? Indeed?" Owlspeak herself, in greener days, hunted bears, killing more than one with her bare arms.

Weedhead nodded. Owlspeak took up more of the girl's hair and cut it off with her knife. The girl did not raise her hand or betray any emotion. Owlspeak finished the job by hacking off a few remaining clumps, and shaving the stubble with a sure and swift hand. The girl was now as bald as a rock. Owlspeak released her.

"A warrior should not wear her hair long," said Owlspeak.

The girl stood and looked at the floor. She did not speak.

"I asked you if you were hungry," said Owlspeak.

"I would not refuse a meal."

"Neither would I. There is smoked meat in the larder. Some eggs and bread. Let's see what you can do with it. I'll expect my breakfast in twenty minutes."

Weedhead betrayed no hint that she resented her treatment or her task. She merely bowed, very slightly, and went to the stove where she began to build up the fire and was soon occupied with the preparation of Owlspeak's meal. Owlspeak sat on the edge of her bed and watched her.

"What do you know of my gift?" she said.

"Your name denotes your gift," said Weedhead as she tossed smoked pork into a pan and shook it over the fire. "You speak with animals and they speak to you." The aroma of finely seared flesh filled Owlspeak's shack, relaxing her defenses just a little. This happened more and more often lately and she knew it to be a symptom of getting older. If she let herself, and she usually chose not to, she could easily wallow in pity at not having been killed in battle. That would have been a much more agreeable fate than this extended slip into weakness.

"Indeed I do as you say," said Owlspeak. "And what do you know of the transfer of this gift?"

"The legend is that only one warrior may possess it at any one time. That the passing on of the gift is not through the possessor's offspring. Usually if falls to whoever kills the possessor, but the possessor may, at her discretion, pass it on to a favored recipient. A kiss, so the legend goes."

"The legend is correct. I received the gift from an old woman when I had only as many years as you. She kissed me and a world opened up to me."

Weedhead nodded. "This tale is known by many."

"And now," said Owlspeak, "you wish to have that world opened to you."

"I do. I promise, if I am chosen, to treat the gift with reverence."

"You realize that having the gift makes you a target. Everyone will want to slay you."

"As they have wanted to slay you," said Weedhead.

"As you could, if you so chose, attempt to slay me now," said Owlspeak.

"It is as you say, but such an action would be criminal. I am not a criminal."

Weedhead cracked eggs into the pan with the frying pork and stirred the mixture around with a wooden spoon. She rummaged in drawers, apparently looking for some kitchen utensil. Owlspeak thought to give her direction, but then chose not to. Weedhead shrugged and pulled her own knife from her holder, strapped, as Owlspeak's had been, around her thigh, and carved off four slabs of bread from the loaf on the counter. She scraped the contents of the pan onto the slices, then slapped the bread onto plates and walked over to Owlspeak and handed her one of the plates.

Owlspeak took the food. She was surprised that she had an appetite.

"I'm dying," said Owlspeak. "Some morbid rot inside me, eating away my guts."

"I know," said Weedhead. "I'm here to ease your burden."

LATER THAT DAY, fortified by Weedhead's meal, Owlspeak went outside for the first time in weeks and sat under a tree in the woods surrounding her house. She waited for birds to come and before long a cardinal lighted beside her.

"What ho?" said Owlspeak to the shimmering red bird. The cardinal looked up at Owlspeak and regarded her with curiosity.

You understand me? came a voice in Owlspeak's head, the cardinal's voice.

"Yes," said Owlspeak. "What can you tell me of the countryside? Is there peace over the land? Are there armies amassing against us?"

You ask many questions.

"You need only answer the ones you choose."

Of opposing armies, I see none. Of peace, I see plenty. In you, I see distress.

"Do not trouble yourself with my trials. What can you tell me of my visitor? Did she indeed come from Gilderdale?"

I saw her days ago. She was determined to find you, it seems.

Before Owlspeak could ask any more questions, the cardinal, apparently needing to attend to other business, spread his wings and flew up. Owlspeak watched him as long as she could, until he disappeared against the sky. She sighed. No one, neither human nor animal, wanted to be around her in her diseased condition.

No one except Weedhead. Very well, thought Owlspeak, I will put her to work.

The subsequent week saw Weedhead scrape moss off Owlspeak's roof, gather the last of the harvest from her garden, caulk gaps in Owlspeak's walls, chop and stack several cords of wood for the winter, and, in general, help get the place looking like it belonged to someone with at least a little sense of order and style.

"I don't know why I'm having you do all this," said Owlspeak. "I don't think I'll last until spring."

Pain gripped her constantly, the rot growing inside her. This was nothing. She could endure pain if she had to, and she had, many times in the past. It was not the pain that troubled her but what the pain indicated: that her days were most likely numbered.

"You're getting your house in order," said Weedhead. "Every creature wants to leave things better than when they came in."

"What do you know of creatures and their desires?" said Owlspeak.

"I know when they want to kill me, and I kill them first."

Owlspeak shook her head. "No creature *wants* to kill you. Some do so out of instinct. But instinct is not desire. That curse befalls only our kind."

"And how can you be sure," said Weedhead.

"The gift, remember?"

"I have lived with you for seven days," said Weedhead.

"Yes. And?"

"May I be permitted to speak freely?"

"When have I stopped you?"

Weedhead was about to speak up, but Owlspeak waved her hand. "Never mind. What do you have to say to me?"

"With all the respect due an elder and heroic warrior, I would, most humbly, suggest that you perhaps could have done more with your gift."

"I saved the land," said Owlspeak. "What more would you have me do? What more could anyone do?"

"Creature still fights against creature. Blood is still spilled for no reason. It seems to me that you might have forged some kind of peace in the animal kingdom."

Owlspeak's heart felt as though it had been kicked by a bear, then stomped on by pigs. She had begun to feel as though this girl might be worthy to take her gift, then this. Peace in the animal kingdom? She was either full of youthful naiveté, or she was mad. Possibly both.

"You speak nonsense," said Owlspeak. "There can be no peace between those who require one another's flesh for their sustenance."

Weedhead held up her hand and brought the index finger of her other hand to her lips. Her eyes darted from side to side and she tilted her head toward the door. "There's someone out there," she whispered.

"They've come for me," said Owlspeak. "Just as you did."

"But they do not come openly. They skulk. I feel their footprints, the vibrations."

"They?" whispered Owlspeak.

"At least two of them. Possibly three."

Owlspeak rose from her sitting position and went to a wall where her sword rested, waiting. She took it by the handle and hefted it, trying to get in sync with its energy. It felt so heavy. Was there a time she held two of these, one in each hand, and wielded them both with gusto? There was, but she could hardly conceive of who she was then, who she had to be, so different from herself now, to take such actions.

Weedhead sprang to her feet with her sword held high above her head and took only a couple of steps to get to the door. She swung it open and stood in the doorway. The sun had long set. Stars sparkled around her silhouette, backlit by dim moonlight.

"Who prowls and sneaks about like a coward?" asked Weedhead of the night air. "Show yourselves or be cursed to hell, the lot of you."

Silence from the night. Owlspeak wondered if there really was anyone there. She had felt no vibrations in the floor, but then, her powers of perception were not what they had been. All her senses were fading.

"What do you see?" she asked Weedhead.

The girl shook her head. "Nothing," she whispered. "So far."

Presently some rustling in the bushes and feet stepping on dry leaves. Owlspeak saw the outlines of three figures emerge from the woods. Her respect for Weedhead instantly doubled.

"We have no quarrel with you," said one of the figures. A man's voice. Young. Did Owlspeak detect a hint of fear? Some trembling, yes, but was it merely from exertion? She couldn't tell.

"Indeed you do have a quarrel with me," said Weedhead. "You trespass on my land."

"This is not your land. We know the old lady lives here. Give her to us and we will leave in peace. Resist us, and we will kill you too."

Why did the cardinal not warn Owlspeak of these criminals, these would-be murderers? Did she not ask the right questions? They are not an army, but they manifestly *are* her enemy. They just said as much. She shook her head. Foolish old lady. Perhaps she should let them kill her. Put the whole business of life behind her, once and for all.

Weedhead still held her sword high. She took one small step forward, called to the spirits to protect her, and then ran at the three with all her might and speed, swinging her sword as she went. The three, perhaps startled by her zeal, were slow in reacting. They did not retreat quickly enough and did not step aside smartly. Weedhead's blade caught one of the vermin directly on the neck. A muffled cry, tinged with gurgling came from him as he fell to his knees and clutched at his throat. Owlspeak, by this time, had herself advanced toward the door, sword held as high as she could manage. Weedhead wasted no time finishing off her first victim. He bled his life into the ground while Weedhead's blade rose up and arced down toward one of the other intruders, who had the wherewithal to raise his own sword. The night air rang with the clash of metal. Weedhead struck his sword again, and a third time. Meanwhile, the third trespasser, who had stumbled back in fear when Weedhead had run toward them, tried to lift himself up from the ground, but was obviously unnerved by the sight of his comrade's gushing arteries soaking the earth. Owlspeak took the opportunity to advance on him. He lifted his sword, but his hands trembled. A frightened assassin, such a pitiful sight. Owlspeak knocked the sword out of his hand. It went skittering through the leaves, a kind of crunching sound.

"You would kill me?" said Owlspeak. "You, who cannot quell your own fears. You would dispatch me and take my gift?"

The man, for he was a man, no mere child, raised his clasped hands and begged Owlspeak for mercy.

"I will give you mercy," said Owlspeak. "I will make your death painless."

With effort, she pulled her sword up and brought it down, swiftly, with gravity's help, onto the man's neck. There was some resistance, but not enough. Owlspeak's sword went through his neck like a knife through pig fat. His head rolled onto the ground and his torso geysered briefly, then fell over.

She turned her attention to Weedhead, now fully engaged with the last adversary, grunting with every swing of her blade. The man, easily twice the size of Weedhead, had met his match and he knew it. His eyes were wild and full of fear. A cowardly look. It disgusted Owlspeak. She thought to help Weedhead by dispatching the scum from behind, but decided the girl did not need her help. She had an inferior sword, and she was out weighed, but that did not matter. She fought with skill and valor, pushing the man back toward the forest from where he had come. Finally, with nothing left in him, he could not lift his feet high enough and he stumbled and fell. He tried to raise his sword up against Weedhead, but he was so weakened that he could not muster the strength. Weedhead, with a colossal grunt, struck the sword from his hand. It fell to the ground and a split second later her blade entered the man's sternum. She pushed on the handle, hard, and must have pierced his heart. Blood gushed from his mouth and splashed over his chin and down to Weedhead's blade. Weedhead placed her foot on the man's chest, directly in his spilled blood, and yanked her blade out. He fell over, a blank and dead look in his eyes.

Weedhead turned to Owlspeak, panting. Sweat poured from her forehead.

"You get some interesting visitors." she said.

Owlspeak nodded. Her head felt light. The stars above her apparently did not approve of her exertions, for they spun in ever more rapid circles until they swirled into bright rings and then darkened as Owlspeak's knees gave way and she fell to the ground in a faint.

WHY BRING ME here? Who is this person?

A voice, gravelly and small, entered Owlspeak's consciousness. The air above her, foggy and studded with cracks, like warped wood, resolved into her shack's ceiling and she realized she was on her back in her bed. A stabbing pain drilled itself into her belly. Her mouth filled with saliva and she lifted her head from her repose, leaned over, and spat on the floor.

Hey, watch it.

The gravelly voice. She glanced over and saw a squirrel. It sat on the floor and regarded her with big brown eyes.

"What are you doing here?" said Owlspeak.

Your friend brought me here. I think she thought I might be able to wake you. Took long enough. I've been trying to talk to you for days.

"Days? How many days."

What does it matter? You talk to us, to animals such as me?

"Yup," said Owlspeak. "It's a gift. So they tell me."

Now I've seen everything. Now I can die.

"You will. In a year or two. Count on it."

Not before you, from what I hear.

Owlspeak rolled back until her spine and shoulder blades touched her mattress again. She could not bear this creature any longer. She could not bear the words of any creature anymore. Time to let all this go.

The door swung open. "Ah." Weedhead's voice. "You're awake."

Tell her I want to go now. I've done my job.

Yes, of course. "Let the squirrel out," said Owlspeak.

Weedhead swung the door open. The squirrel's tiny feet scraped along the floor and then she was gone. Weedhead came and kneeled next to Owlspeak.

"I have some soup for you," she said. "To help get your strength back."

"My strength isn't coming back," said Owlspeak.

"It will."

"It won't. What did you do with those assassins?"

"Would-be assassins," said Weedhead.

"Very well," said Owlspeak. "Would-be assassins."

"I dragged their carcasses to the woods. Vermin will dispose of them."

"You are a fierce fighter for someone who wants to bring harmony to the animal kingdom. How do you reconcile such divergent capacities?"

"I do not deny the necessity of defending oneself from predators. I wish to bring a world into being in which there are no predators. I believe your gift will help me to communicate to all the creatures, to make them understand the value of cooperation and peace. Harmony. There is no need to kill others."

"I see," said Owlspeak. Weedhead rose from her knees and went to the stove where a big pot of soup simmered. She dipped a ladle into the pot and poured a good portion of soup into a bowl then brought it to Owlspeak.

"It's got meat in it," said Weedhead. "And potatoes. Good things to revive you."

"Did you convince the meat to jump into the soup?"

"Hera," said Weedhead, "I don't have all the answers. I don't pretend I do. But I want to try. The spilling of blood is not good for anyone."

The girl had a point, but how could one person, even with the gift, change the world? It didn't seem possible. "I don't need reviving," said Owlspeak. "I have a task for you."

Weedhead put down the bowl, reluctantly, then bowed her head. "What task?" she asked.

"Kill me," said Owlspeak.

"No!" said Weedhead.

"I know you can do it. I saw you swing your sword. If you kill me, my gift becomes yours."

"That is not the only way. You can give it to me."

"Yes yes, and then what? You will leave me. I will be alone, waiting for the rot to consume me. What good am I like this? I cannot fight without fainting. I cannot care for myself any longer. I need you to feed me. I have been a warrior all my life. I understand no other way."

"You ask me to commit murder."

"I ask you to commit an act of mercy. Others will come to attack me. You cannot fight them all."

"I have already. Two came yesterday."

"You slew them?"

"Of course."

"Then slay me. Now. Release us both from the burden of my infirmity."

"Hera," said Weedhead. "I cannot. Ask me anything, but not that."

Owlspeak's lips trembled. One kiss on this young woman's lips and she would see the world as Owlspeak saw it. One kiss.

"If you do not want to help me," said Owlspeak. "Then go. Leave my home. I don't want you here."

"But Hera," said Weedhead. "You are weak."

"And what of it?" said Owlspeak.

"If you send me away, you will die."

"I will die either way. Quickly or slowly, what is it to you?"

"Your gift . . ."

"I already told you. The gift is yours for the taking. Raise your sword and be done with it."

Owlspeak studied Weedhead's face. She looked to be in some difficulty, as though she was actually considering Owlspeak's request. Owlspeak allowed herself the thrill of imagining Weedhead's sword swooping through the air and connecting with her neck. She savored the anticipation of severing her life from this world. She wanted the release. Savored the chance to be delivered from pain and shame.

But no. Weedhead rose and shook her head emphatically. "No, Hera. I cannot."

She stepped back. Owlspeak picked up the bowl of soup and

flung it at the young woman, who did not attempt to dodge it. The bowl hit her knee. Soup splashed onto the floor. It looked like vomit. A sour taste invaded Owlspeak's mouth.

"Every warrior should accept their fruits of battle," said Owlspeak. "Your reward for saving my life was my gift. If you are too much a coward to take it, then leave me. Go."

Weedhead did not utter a word. She turned from Owlspeak and put on her sheepskin coat and shouldered her bag and retrieved her sword from its resting place near the door.

"Good bye, Hera," she said.

Owlspeak did not answer her. The cold overwhelmed her. She wanted to sink deeper under her covers and find some warmth. Any warmth. She turned on her side and brought her knees up to her chest and wrapped her arms around her legs.

She had only one thing left to do now. She needed to gather whatever strength remained to carry out one last task for herself.

SHE SLEPT THE remainder of the day and through the next night. Toward morning the lightening sky seemed to crawl into her shack and drape itself across her face. She blinked her eyes open and exerted her will and pushed herself out of her bed and stepped onto the floor. She was woozy and wobbly, but she had enough in her to do what needed to be done. She walked with an unsteady gait, doubled over from the pain in her belly, and made her way out the door and stood facing the woods. Darkness in there.

What is wrong with you? You are not well. Go back to your nest, woman.

The voices of birds. Incessant chatter. She would be well rid of them in a short time.

She shambled to the trees where she smelled the rotting flesh of the dead men. As she walked, she put her hand on tree trunks for support. Was this any way for a warrior to die?

She shook her head, not wanting to think too hard about her former glories. That was in the past. Who cared of such things now?

The girl, Weedhead, had dragged the men to a small clearing. Owlspeak now saw their bones, still wet. Birds had been on the corpses. Bears too, it seemed. She saw their tracks. Felt their presence. They would return. Still plenty of meat on those bones. Everything in the forest gets used up. Nothing wasted.

She was having difficulty keeping on her feet. She crouched down and put her palms on the forest floor and made progress on her hands and knees. To die among her vanquished enemies. It would not be such a bad thing. To die at the jaws of a bear. It felt right and proper.

She pulled herself along the ground until she had no more strength and collapsed onto her belly. Then she rolled over and looked up at the sky. It was not fully bright yet. There were still some stars visible. Better here. Better beneath the sparkle and glint of stars than beneath her wretched roof.

"Come get me," she said. She tried to shout the words, but they dribbled out of her mouth in a whisper.

She strained to hear a response.

You are old. Who would want to eat you?

That was a bear. Owlspeak felt a rush of elation.

"I have killed your kind," said Owlspeak. "Here is a chance for revenge. Have at me."

Woman, do you wish to die?

"It is time. Yes. I wish to die. I have no fight in me. Not anymore."

She heard a crunch of leaves and a snap of branches. Heavy feet behind her, out of her vision, feet that had to belong to a large beast. A roar. Elation filled her heart. The bear circled around and approached her from the side. It looked female. A handsome creature, full brown fur, mouth dripping with juices. She paused, as though savoring the thought of chomping into Owlspeak.

"My neck please," said Owlspeak. "Do not dither. Take me swiftly."

Do not tell me how to go about attaining my sustenance, woman. I have my ways.

The bear took a step forward. Then another. Owlspeak gritted her teeth. She would have to accept her fate now. Nothing to be done.

The bear reared back and opened its jaws as wide as it could. Owlspeak saw its red tongue and its yellow teeth and expected that next it would clamp its jaws on her, but instead it kept going back and back, until it stumbled and tried to turn around in mid air. It could not. It had a sword stuck in its spine, directly between its shoulders.

Oh oh oh. What is this? What is this in me?

A foot came up from somewhere out of Owlspeak's range of view. A human foot. Weedhead's foot. It planted itself in the bear's fur, right next to the blade of the sword, and then the sword slid out of the wound, as it had slid out of the man's chest only days ago. The blade was covered in blood. Dripping with blood. The sight of it roused Owlspeak to cry out.

"Hera," said Weedhead. "Calm yourself. I would not let you die by the tooth of a beast such as this."

Owlspeak watched as Weedhead approached her.

"You dare to deprive me of my last dignity," said Owlspeak, more out of sorrow than anger. More out of weariness.

Weedhead bent down next to Owlspeak.

"I wish your gift," said Weedhead. "With it I can bring peace to the land."

"You are a farmer from Gilderdale," said Owlspeak. "Soft. You don't know the first thing about being a warrior."

Weedhead parted her lips and bent down close to Owlspeak's mouth.

A voice came to her. Many voices. The creatures of the forest in a chorus, a sustained call to one of their own.

She offers you release. Take it. Take it.

Weedhead hovered over Owlspeak.

Owlspeak raised her chin until her lips met Weedhead's. They kissed for what seemed a long time. An eternity. Owlspeak's life filled her vision: the battles, the blood, the voices. The fading voices.

Take it. Take it. Take it take it . . .

Until she heard nothing. Only her own heart, beating like mad. The blood rushing through her veins. This was the way to end it, wasn't it? This was the way to die.

Weedhead rose to her feet. Her mouth wide open, she flung her hands out and bent her neck back so the sky seemed to pour into her. Owlspeak shed tears until the sky became a blur.

"I hear them," said Weedhead. "I hear them all. The animals, they speak to me."

"I'm glad," said Owlspeak.

Weedhead looked down at Owlspeak. "Thank you," she said.

Owlspeak said nothing more. She had nothing left in her. No words. No will. No life.

Weedhead lifted her sword up, high against the sky, then swung it down, swift and sure, on a flight from whatever providence might exist to a rendezvous with Owlspeak's throat.

O Negative

I CAN'T STAND the sight of my own blood, so I never watch when they take it. I know they stick a needle in my arm, and I know the tube that trails that needle turns crimson, and I know the bag at the end of the tube fills up with this deeply red, almost black, liquid.

My liquid.

But I never watch it. I happened to glance at it once, and I passed out. They had to revive me with smelling salts, which is no way to wake up. It shocks you. Makes you think you're in the wrong world. Maybe in the wrong universe.

But I do it. My name's Max. I donate every three months, like clockwork. I close up my food cart if I have to. I lose the income for those couple of hours, just so I can donate the blood that society needs. Sometimes I donate more often than every three months. You have to be crafty about it, though. If you go too often, they start to notice. You have to go to different places and fool them into believing you haven't donated in the past three months.

They have a rule. I guess it's not good to donate more often. Your body doesn't have a chance to replenish itself if you donate too often. That's what they say, anyway. I've never had a problem. My body makes blood like there's no tomorrow.

I have about six or seven donation centers I go to around the city. I especially like to donate on cold days. It warms me up to think someone is going to be saved with my blood. That's the thrill, really. I'm like a reverse vampire. They like to take blood. I like to give it.

Not that I think vampires are real. They're not. I'm pretty sure. Though sometimes I wonder. Some of the people who come to my cart, well, from the look of them, you'd swear they had this *way* about them. They're eating my food, but they'd much rather be consuming, well, something *else*.

At one of the donation centers, there's this lovely woman. Her name tag says her name is Julia. Pretty name. Matches her. She's good with the needle. One of the best. I can barely feel it piercing my skin. She's about my age, and she always has a nice smile for me. I don't think she remembers my name or anything, but she's very welcoming. It's like I make her day every time I come there. Other places, I'll let the months slide by a little, just so they don't get to be suspicious of me. But at her station, I make sure I'm there on a quarterly basis. I come on the solstices and equinoxes. Makes it easy to remember. Ties my donation habit to the heavens, which makes it kind of cosmic.

I'm O negative. If you know anything about blood, you know they love O neg at the donation centers. I'm the universal donor. Anyone can use my blood. I remember when I first found out I was an O neg. I was in middle school. We had this project in science class where all the pupils pricked their fingers and dripped a couple of drops of blood onto a slide. Then the science teacher had us put the blood in a test tube with some solution or other, swished some chemicals into it, then dipped a slip of paper into the test tube. Something like that. The paper turned color. You compared the color to a chart to see what blood type you were. I was one of only two negs, and the only O neg. The teacher said I had very useful blood.

Very useful blood.

Teachers don't know the influence they have. I still remember that phrase. I remembered it for a long time. Years. I rolled it over in my head. It had a certain musical quality to my ear. It was as though *I* was useful. As though my own blood made *me* an important person. From that early age, I thought my blood was going to be my life. Or at least, make my life useful.

Did I mention that Julia has the most beautiful hair? It's not quite black and not quite auburn. Something in-between. I don't think it's colored. I think it's natural. Although I couldn't really say for sure. She wears earrings that match her hair. She's very aware of her hair. Sometimes, on hot days, she wears it wound up on top of her head. Other times it brushes the tops of her shoulders.

Once I complimented her on her hair. She took it well, I thought. Didn't think I was weird or anything. She said she liked my hair, too, and then we both laughed.

Look, I don't want you to think I'm creepy. And now I'm sorry I even brought up Julia's hair. It's not like I don't think of her as a real person. The thing is, Julia is very comfortable around me. Very comfortable. If she wasn't, she'd make sure someone else was on duty when I came in. Really. I'm completely predictable.

Like, every summer solstice, I'm there with my sleeve rolled up, ready to give blood. Every winter solstice. Spring and Autumnal equinox. She knows that. She could have someone else draw the blood from me on those days. It would be a simple matter. There are other phlebotomists on duty. But she doesn't. That's important, I think.

I asked her once how many people had my blood in them. I asked her in a casual kind of way, like I was just making conversation. She thought about it. Well, she said, how many times have you donated?

I had to be careful not to give her the real number. I'm thirty-eight, I said. I've been donating since I was twenty-one. Four times a year.

She smiled. That's real dedication.

Especially for someone who can't stand the sight of blood.

Yes, she said. Especially.

So, I said. That's 17 years of donating. 17 times 4 is 68. That means 68 people have some of my blood in them.

It's probably less than that, she said.

Oh?

Sometimes we don't get to use the blood that's donated. There's no demand for it and it goes bad.

Goes bad? I said. Really?

I know it's disappointing, she said. But it's actually a good thing. It means we had more on hand than we needed. Better to have a surplus than a shortage.

Right, I said. That's a good way to look at it. That way no one who needs it doesn't get it.

She patted my hand. Exactly, she said.

I saw her logic and it made sense, but I was still disappointed. I didn't want to think of my own blood as getting old. Going past its expiration date like some moldy cheese in the fridge.

You seem upset, she said.

I hated that she noticed that. I wanted her to think I understood the ins and outs of blood donation. I wanted her to think of me as a professional. Someone able to control his emotions.

It's nothing, I said.

Everything okay?

Inside, I appreciated the sympathy. On the outside, I tried to project this demeanor of not *needing* sympathy. I'm not sure I succeeded at all. Julia is very astute.

Even if it's not used, she said, it's not completely lost. When blood gets to be about three months old they can take the plasma out of it and store that. Plasma lasts a long time.

But it's not as useful as blood, is it? I said.

No, she said, reluctantly. She didn't want me to feel bad. She was concerned for me.

Still, I said, as though I was trying to cheer *her* up. It's good that I donate. *Usually* my blood gets used.

I could tell she was ready to move on. She had put the needle in, and given me the rubber ball to squeeze in my hand, and there were other people waiting in line to donate that she had to get to. I didn't want to seem needy, so I didn't keep her any longer.

She went to one of the other lounge chairs and talked to the person there in the same reassuring tone she always used with me. That's the way it is with Julia. She is polite to everyone. I think this is one of the best things about her. I'm not really that special to her. I'm just as important as everyone else in the world.

I HAVE A food cart in the city. I serve healthy food. Mostly vegetable wraps and some roasted chicken wraps. I use tortillas that I make myself and I'm very careful to steam the vegetables. No oils or sugars.

My cart does pretty good business.

A lot of people, when they place their orders, they're standing in front of me talking on their smart phones. They got important things to discuss. They don't have time to hang up just to order their food. So they gesture at the menu while they're talking and I make them what they pointed at and hand it to them while all the while they're still talking on their phones.

It's funny, really. It's the comedy of daily life. I find it very amusing they think what they put in their bodies is less important than the words they say. Words disappear into the air. Food *becomes* your body. Which means it's actually kind of important.

Anyway, that's how I first heard about the shooting across town. A guy pointed at a picture of the number 4 wrap. He had his ear on his phone and I could hear someone screaming on the other end the whole time I was making his wrap.

What's going on? I asked him as I gave him his plate.

Some guy shot up a school, he said, as though he was telling me the weatherman was expecting some rain tomorrow.

What school? I said.

He shrugged. Don't know it. Across town somewhere. Sounds pretty bad.

I closed up my cart and took the bus to the nearest donation center. Any time there's a bad thing like a shooting or some other disaster where people get injured or hurt, they'll need blood. I've learned that in my years donating blood. And as I told you already, I'm an O neg. They always want O negs.

The bus dropped me off a few blocks from the donation center. It was a small building. Used to be a house, now it has some medical offices, a dentist, things like that. I walked as fast as I could, then broke into a little bit of a trot. As I got closer, I saw there was a crowd of people around the entrance to the building. They were holding up signs and had linked themselves across the entrance. I couldn't tell what the signs were, but I could see the people were angry. They were shouting slogans and some of them had their fists raised in the air.

I didn't like the look of things. Not one little bit. I could tell something was terribly wrong.

As I got closer I saw one of the signs. It said NO BLOOD FOR BLOOD. That seemed strange. Another sign, held by someone else, had SACRIFICE IS GOD'S WISDOM.

I got this really queasy feeling in my stomach, like things were too dangerous for me to be there. The hair on my neck prickled at me, and I felt like my head was too hot, like I was going to overheat and scald my own blood. It felt dangerous.

I angled my trot toward the entrance to the donation center, but one of the sign holders stepped in front of me. She was a younger woman, maybe twenty-five or so. She had wild hair and these kind of eyes I can't describe—they looked crazed, like she could take a bite out of your face with her eyelids. Like her eyelids had teeth.

I stopped, then tried to go around her, but she stepped in front of me again. Behind her, the steps to the entrance were narrow and lined with hand rails. I couldn't get past her.

What's going on? I asked.

We're keeping people from donating blood, she said. She was just as calm as you please.

What? I said. Why? Don't you know there are people shot? They're going to need blood.

Of course we know, she said. That's why we're here. Bleeding hearts come out after every shooting. Trying to save the world. She stepped back from me and spit on the ground to show her disgust.

Some of her comrades in this insanity clustered around her and glared at me.

Keep your blood, they said. God gave it to you. It's not for anyone else.

One of these crazies, with a big white sign splattered with red paint—to look like blood—got too close to me, trying to push me back the way I came. I wasn't about to be pushed. I stood my ground.

The police will be here soon, I said. They won't let you block this entrance.

The police, she said. Ha! The police are all at the scene of the shooting. Many kids dead, many more injured and bleeding. They're the worst bleeding hearts of all, the police. They aren't going to care what goes on here. At least not for a while.

Was she right? I didn't know. People were still advancing on me. I felt like a fly in a spider's web. The man who told me to get out dropped his sign and put up his arms and crossed them in front of his chest and advanced toward me. I put my arms up in the same way and met him with hard contact.

You ready to rumble? he asked.

I didn't answer. I was bigger than him, so I braced myself on one foot and pushed him as hard as I could. He fell back, right on his ass end. He didn't appear hurt. Or particularly distressed. He looked up at me from the pavement and grinned, like this was the best time of his life.

Then the rest of them swarmed over me. I tried to fight back. I swung a fist or two, but there were too many. They threw me to the ground and kicked me. I covered my face and head as best I could. They concentrated on my body, kicking my stomach and chest. They tried for my crotch, but I was curled up too much for that.

A couple of them swung at me with their signs. They connected on my hands and my face. Blood spurted from my fingers and around my cheek and temple. The hot liquid felt something like fire coursing over my skin.

I was on fire. Or my blood was. I couldn't tell. I was too

confused to understand what was happening. I screamed at them to stop. They didn't. They were having too much fun, and the sight of my O neg, so rich and red, got their bloodlust going.

Eventually, though, they stepped away. I heard panting breaths, some laughs, the slapping of hands. I couldn't look up, but I imagined them high-fiving each other in triumph, like they had scored the winning touchdown. I groaned and tried to move, but everything hurt. I heard footsteps. Someone running down the wooden steps. I dared to pull my hands down from my head and tried to straighten myself out. My tongue tasted dirt and concrete. I spit out the grit. It was mixed with blood. I had bruises all over my body and I was pretty sure things were broken. I looked up at the sky. The sun beat down on me.

God didn't want this blood to drain out of me here, I said.

A necessary sacrifice, said one of them. Drained here or drained in there. You were going to break a natural law, one way or the other. We just did it quicker, and no one is going to benefit.

The running steps slowed down and I felt hands on my chest and face. Her hands. Julia. I recognized them immediately.

Oh my God, she said. What happened here? Max?

My name sounded like music in her mouth. Are you okay? she asked. Max?

But before I could answer she was yanked away from me by two of the protesters. They grabbed her arms and pulled her back. She struggled against them. I admired her fight. She wasn't going to let them have their way without a battle. She kicked and tried to take her hands back. She was a ball of energy, flailing in all directions. Let me down! she said. Let me down you crazies.

We will let you down if you promise not to help this man. Or anyone.

What?

Promise.

She stopped flailing. She stilled her arms and legs. She looked bewildered, like someone had taken the spit right out of her.

They don't want anyone helping anyone else, I said. My voice was broken. It felt like my vocal chords were sifting gravel. The words were hard on my throat. I could barely make them crawl out of my lungs and through my mouth.

That can't be, she said. No one would protest that.

The woman I first encountered stepped close to Julia. You need to know something, she said. It's not just here. We have people all over town. We're blocking entrances to hospitals and clinics and doctor offices, not just donation centers. We are determined to stop the epidemic of sacrifice that annuls or belittles the sacrifice that God has decreed.

You see? I said.

You people are crazy, said Julia.

We're not asking you to understand, said the woman. Not everyone does. But we have thought about this for a long time. This shooting is our chance to get our message out.

What message? said Julia. That helping people is *bad?*

Precisely.

Neither of us, not me or Julia, had an answer to that because any answer seemed self-evident and these people were obviously not interested in self-evident truths.

Julia pointed to my head. He's hurt, she said. If he doesn't receive aid, he'll only get worse.

His own fault, said the woman.

No, said Julia. She looked at me with such pity in her eyes. I felt a connection to her. It was as though our souls had met and forged another soul, one bigger than the both of us put together.

I don't expect you to understand, said Julia, but blood does that to people. It brings them together. The most intimate connections are made in the furnace of conflict. Soldiers bond over blood. They use wounds to find a life bigger than could ever seem possible.

I sat up. My head hurt. It felt like several dozen creatures with hammers were working away in my skull, trying to find a way to excavate my thoughts with force if necessary.

I put my hand out to Julia. She reached for me. The people holding her didn't stop her. My fingers touched her fingers. My skin brushed against her skin. Our essences met and curled around each other. My heart, beating like crazy, strong as a locomotive engine, also felt like it was going to melt. Like it *had* melted and I was now being sustained only by a strange will that, disembodied from my form, seemed to find some exalted place from which to observe Julia's singular beauty as a human being.

Blood still flowed from my wounds. It pulsed across my skin. It soaked into my shirt. I felt the fabric clinging wetly and hotly to my skin.

What if I don't do anything but clean him up? said Julia. I won't draw blood from him, and I won't put any blood in him. I'll just stop the flow.

Some of the protesters gathered into a tight little circle and tilted their heads together. Their little powwow went on for a while. In the meantime I met Julia's concerned gaze with complete courage and bravery. I lifted up my head, as though I was gesturing to the angels in the sky.

I put my tongue out of my mouth and probed the spot where my lower and upper lips met on my right side. An amalgam of tears, mucous, and blood flowed onto my tongue. I flicked it back and swallowed it. Nothing had ever lifted my spirits as much as the taste of that mixture.

Very well, said one of the protesters. We think maybe we went a little too far with this man. You may tend to his wounds but no blood will be transferred either into him or out of him. We'll send in one of our people to make sure.

Julia bent down and grabbed me by the armpits and tried to lift me, but I was too heavy for her and had to help her by pushing myself up on my palms and raising my body to a standing position. I leaned on her, but not too much, as we both negotiated the steps, gingerly and one at a time.

The woman I first encountered trailed behind us. I could hear her disgusted remarks as we walked. She said I was weak and contemptible. She said I had no integrity and that people like me were the problem with the world. We expected others to take care of us.

I didn't answer. My head was pounding and that was the least of it. The bruises hurt like hell. My belly was a ball of pain. My limbs felt like there were breaks in them. Julia countered the protester's words with soothing words of her own. She assured me everything was going to be fine. She told me we were almost there.

We entered the donation room. Several chairs were arranged in a row, just as I remember them. I should really be calling an ambulance, said Julia. You need more care than I can give.

No ambulance, said the protestor woman. No outside aid.

All of you are in trouble, said Julia. All of you will go to jail.

Don't count on it, said the woman. We won't be here long enough to get arrested. We'll disappear.

With Julia's assistance, we got close enough to one of the chairs so that I could fall into it. Nothing felt as good as slipping into that comfort. I sighed as I adjusted myself on the comfy cushions of that chair.

Julia went to the bathroom and returned with a small bowl filled with water, and a cloth. She wet the cloth and began cleaning my head. It hurt when she got close to the cut. The cloth turned red with my blood and then Julia dipped the cloth in the water and the water took on a pinkish tinge. I started crying, seeing my blood wasted like this.

Julia tried to be as cheerful as possible. She kept telling me everything was going to be fine. The protestor, meanwhile, went around the room destroying the equipment. She pulled out boxes of needles and turned the boxes over so the needles scattered around the floor. Then she stepped on them, crushing them. She took a knife and punctured dozens of blood bags. She turned over the stands that held those bags. The clattering was jarring and made me flinch. Julia bent down so she was close to my ear.

It's okay, Max, she said. It's just noise. It isn't going to hurt you.

I was in shock, I guess. The assault on me was like nothing I had ever experienced before. It made me feel as though I was nothing but a bag of blood myself. Something to be punctured and drained. I shivered. Julia reached under the chair and retrieved a blanket.

Are you cold? she asked.

I nodded and she put the blanket over me. By the time she was done cleaning my wounds, the woman appeared to be done destroying donation equipment.

Well, that's that, said the woman. Everything's wrecked. We have struck a blow for nature.

Nature? said Julia.

We were never supposed to go against the will of natural law, said the woman. Don't you know that?

Julia found some alcohol and bandages that the woman had not destroyed. She applied alcohol to my wounds. It stung, then felt good, like I was being cleansed of something awful I didn't understand. Julia bandaged my cuts. Even the adhesive of the bandages felt good, like it was caressing my skin. I imagined my blood seeping into the bandage and staining it. I wanted to look at myself.

Can I have a mirror? I asked Julia.

A mirror? said the protesting woman. What do you want a mirror for?

He wants to see what he looks like, said Julia. Is that against your beliefs?

The protesting woman shook her head. Julia left my side to retrieve a mirror from somewhere. As soon as she left, I felt like I was the most lonely person in the world. I called to the protester woman. What's your name? I asked.

She shook her head. No names, she said. I don't want you to identify me later.

That's ridiculous, I said. You were outside. In public. People are going to recognize you. Everyone is going to recognize you.

I don't care, she said.

Come here and hold my hand, please. I wanted to get that sentence out without tears, but my voice quavered. Her face softened, a little. I saw that perhaps there was a real human being behind the façade. Was it possible? I wasn't sure. Her actions indicated she was so far gone from normal behavior that she might have been an alien. Maybe *had* to be something from some other place.

I don't know, she said.

It won't cost you anything, I said. Just come hold my hand. I'm scared.

She hesitated another second then walked over and took my hand. She held it lightly, but it was enough. It calmed me. Made me see that things might be okay.

I hurt, I said. Or, rather, mumbled. I could hardly get any words out. I did start crying then. Tears and sobs came freely. I tried to hold them at first, but that didn't last. I stopped trying to keep them in and let them do what they wanted. I got blubbery and felt her begin to pull away from me. She didn't want to be around someone like me: sloppy and possibly unstable.

Julia came back holding a framed mirror which I think she must have gotten from one of the bathrooms. She saw me and the protestor woman and I think I saw a hint of jealousy in her eyes, but I could have been wrong. I always had to temper my observations of Julia. I wanted so much from her that sometimes I ascribed actions and motives to her that were not in her heart.

The protestor woman stepped back from me. She released my hand and went to the front window and looked outside. Julia kept the mirror down for a few seconds. You sure you want to see yourself? she asked.

Yes, I said. I wiped tears from my eyes.

Careful, she said. Don't mess up your bandages.

Okay, I said and blinked hard several times and held myself steady and looked straight ahead. She raised the mirror and placed it in front of me. I had time to catch only a fleeting glimpse of myself—head iced with white bandages stained red, a ghastly and alarming sight—when the door burst open and all the protestors poured into the donation room.

They're coming, someone shouted.

Julia dropped the mirror to the floor. It shattered, adding its jagged edges to the mess on the floor already.

Cops are massing at the front, said one of the protesters. We'll escape through the back. The woman who had held my hand glanced in my direction. I wanted to see her as more than someone caught in some dangerous cult, but that's *all* I could see. Nevertheless, I tried to pull her back from the chaos.

Stay here, I said. I realized I couldn't donate blood, but I thought I could still try to help others. I could try to infuse this woman with a love for humanity.

No, she said. My friends need me.

She ran to the back of the building, along with the others. There were about a dozen or so of them. They ran like a heard of animals, their feet thumping and shaking the building. I looked at Julia. This is a terrible mess, she said.

I nodded. I'll help you clean up.

You don't have to. Just stay where you are.

The shot came next. I saw Julia jerk, then her eyes went wide and startled. She fell to the floor. The next instant, or maybe at the same time, I'm not sure, the window at the front of the donation center shattered. I heard the bullet tear through the glass after the bullet had done its damage.

Stay down, I told her as I quickly slipped out of the chair and went down to the floor myself. I was right beside her. Where did it hit you? I asked.

She was in shock. I saw it in her eyes. She didn't know what to do or think. I had a surge of energy course through me. I grabbed her by the arms and looked her in the face. It's going to be okay, I said. You're still breathing. Where does it hurt?

She moved a hand toward her shoulder. I turned her around and looked at her back. Blood stained her blouse. It was thick and dark, like ink. Looks like it got you pretty good, I said.

Above us, a few more shots shattered more glass and hit the walls on the other side of the room. Dust from the walls clouded the air near the holes, which had sprouted like mushrooms on the paint.

Julia shook her head. That's another mess we're going to have to take care of, she said.

I pulled her shirt down and saw a long streak of blood angling over her shoulder blade. I had to think through what I saw, and realized the bullet probably didn't penetrate her flesh. It had grazed her skin and continued on. Probably also in the wall right now, just like the rest of the bullets that had come through the window.

You've got a bad cut, I said. Nothing more.

She nodded.

What's your blood type? I asked.

Why?

You might need some.

She looked scared.

Tell me, I said. You know mine.

I don't know my blood type, she said.

What? You work in a donation center.

I never had it checked.

You don't donate yourself?

No, she said. I'm afraid to. So I work here.

My picture of Julia was crumbling in my mind. She was afraid of donating blood? Afraid of helping people? That made no sense to me. More shots came through the window.

Who's shooting at us? I called to the air. My nerves were a jangle. I didn't want to hear another bullet crash through glass or hit the wall. Behind me the protestors returned to the donation room. They were bent low, keeping under the path of the bullets. They disgusted me and I told them so.

No time for that now, said the woman who had held my hand. We need you to go out and tell them to stop shooting.

You were supposed to go out back, I said.

There's cops there too.

So you're surrounded, I said.

We're surrounded, she said.

They aren't after us, I said.

The woman shook her head with disgust. The bullets flying into this building don't know that.

I saw her point. I asked someone for a cell phone. One of the protestors handed one to me. I dialed 911. A calm voice answered. I told her that we were in the donation center, people were hurt and please stop shooting at us. She said she would convey the message. A short time later, maybe thirty seconds, the bullets stopped crashing through the window. We all kept very quiet as we assessed the silence in the air.

Damn cops, said one of the protestors. Nervous trigger fingers.

Shhh, I said. I held my finger up to my lips.

I don't know what you're worried about. You're going to get out of this. We're probably going to jail.

Serves you right, I said.

We could take these two hostage, said a protestor.

No hostages, said another. God doesn't take hostages.

We're all hostages of God, said another. They got into an argument, whispering harshly to each other. Something about the limits of theological theorizing. I thought it slightly amusing and might have found it hilarious under other circumstances.

You can't know the mind of God, I said. They stopped their whispering and looked at me. I continued. You can't know the reason he gave me all this good blood, I said.

Julia, who had been silently enduring her pain, now grabbed my arm, as though wanting me to stop talking. I wanted to please her. I always wanted to please her. But I didn't do as she wanted. Not then.

God wanted me to give my blood to others, I said. To help them. No one knows why he would do that. No one knows why he would give us blood that wasn't universally compatible. But he did.

One of the male protestors, who had been hanging back in the group for all this time, said he liked the idea of taking hostages. It might give them a chance to get out of this thing alive.

You don't have any weapons, I said. You can't hold hostages without weapons.

Don't count on that, said the man.

Anyway, I said, they aren't going to kill you now. I phoned them. They know the situation.

You didn't tell them we didn't have any weapons, said the man. They don't know you. He came around the group and stood behind me and put his stick, the one that held up the NO BLOOD FOR BLOOD sign, under my chin and pulled it tight against my throat. I felt the coarse grain of the wood on my skin. My heart rate increased. I felt fear grip me. It was as though I had entered the situation anew. Everything was starting all over again.

Julia raised her arm and hit the man across the back of the head. He raised his hand to the spot where Julia connected and rubbed it. Hey, he said. That hurt.

Julia took the stick from his other hand and hit him across the face. The man staggered back. The other protestors surged around Julia and took the stick away.

I ran toward the group, bent my head down low and put my arms out and tackled them all, pushing them in a jumble to the floor. Screams and shouts of alarm and anger rose up from the heap sprawled on the floor. I was right down there with them. My bandage had been torn off and fresh blood dripped from my head.

A loud pop came from outside the building. A split second later a canister of tear gas sailed through the broken window and fell near us.

They don't want to come in after us, said one of the protesters. They think we might be like the shooters at the school. They're afraid of us.

Doesn't matter now, I said. Tear gas is nasty stuff.

The woman who held my hand grabbed the canister and tossed it back through the window. It didn't help because another came in and another. Thick clouds filled the building. My eyes were already stinging. Julia grabbed my arm and pulled me away from the protesters, who were all wailing and crying. They all had their hands buried in their eyes sockets. Julia ran and I ran with her. We went out the back door with our hands raised high.

Don't shoot! we said. Don't shoot!

Maybe we should have stayed in the building and taken our chances with the protestors and the gas. Maybe we should have called before we ran. I have turned over a lot of maybes in my head since that day. No one says we did anything wrong.

Oh, we might have been better off if we crawled out of the house slowly instead of running at full speed, but no one *blamed* us for that. No one said we were incorrect. But no one says the cops did anything wrong, either. So I have always wondered since then how such a wrong turn of events could have occurred if no one behaved incorrectly. No one has been able to explain it to me.

In any case, our calls for restraint went unheeded. Shots came from cops who were crouched behind the open doors of their police cars. Later they said all the cops in the city were on high alert. They thought anyone might be a shooter. Anyone. They had just seen what happened at the school, and it shattered their professionalism. Maybe that was true. Maybe it wasn't.

At first it felt like someone had jerked at my elbow and I almost turned around to see if Julia was grabbing me, but then I realized that wasn't the case at all. A bullet had gone through my arm. It left a hole on one side of my arm and another hole on the other. For a moment, once I realized what had happened, I experienced this quiet sense of peace. The world was silent and I floated on some kind of euphoria. I had survived a bullet through my body.

Then the pain descended. It was so intense that I crumpled on the spot.

I heard two more shots. The official report of the incident, months later, said there were actually three more. But I only heard two. Which means one or two of the shots did not hit a target.

Oh, but that last one. It connected with Julia's belly. I heard her call out. She called my name. I was on the ground but I crawled in her direction. In the direction of her voice. Above me, footsteps pounded the ground. Shapes flew over me toward the house. I heard later that two of the protestors were killed. Two others were injured, and the rest gave up quietly. Or as quietly as possible, given the circumstances.

When I got to Julia, she was shaking, trembling.

Guess it wasn't such a good idea to run, she said.

I put my hand on her belly and held back the blood.

I called for help. We're good people, I said as loudly as I could. We're not criminals. We help people. We're not bad.

PEOPLE DID FINALLY come to help us. We went to the hospital in separate ambulances. I always regretted that. I would have liked to have gone into treatment with Julia by my side.

In the ambulance I told the paramedics that Julia didn't know her blood type. They needed to be careful. I told them I could donate. I wanted to donate. It was my time, anyway.

They shushed me. Politely. But still. It was clear they wanted me to shut up. They made it official by pumping me full of sedatives. I didn't quite black out, but close. I was aware of arriving at the hospital, and barely conscious of being in a whitish room and a doctor leaning over my arm, stitching something. A bag of blood hung off a hook and a tube from it went into my arm.

So I couldn't give anyone blood. I was the one who needed blood. That disappointed me immensely.

As soon as I could say anything, I asked about Julia. They wanted to know if I was a relative.

We're family, I said.

The nurse seemed doubtful, but she told me. I found out later that all the while I was in the hospital, my food cart was being vandalized. First some people painted stuff on the sides. Nasty stuff. Words people shouldn't see.

Then, during the evening, people broke in and stole all the food. I don't begrudge people that. If you need food, you need food. But then they turned everything in the cart over. They upended my toaster oven and stomped on it. They threw all the pans onto the floor. Then they pushed the cart over. It was so damaged that there was no way to restore it.

Much later, after I was mostly recovered, I thought I should start a new cart. Get my life going again, but I had completely lost the urge to do so. I only wanted to sit in one place and contemplate the ways of the universe and sell my blood.

Yes, sell. I didn't want to donate anymore. People were not worth donating to. This was not an easy thing for me to say or think. Not in any way at all. I think what happened to Julia turned me around.

The nurse, after I kept pestering her about Julia, she finally relented and told me what happened to her. Her liver and kidneys were damaged by the bullet, she said.

The *police* bullet, I said.

She nodded. Yes, she said. The police bullet.

She paused for me. To let me gather my strength, I think.

Go on, I said.

She nodded again. It was bad, but the docs were able to help her. They resected the damaged areas and she's going to be okay.

I was expecting her to tell me Julia was gone. It took me a while for the information to seep into my brain.

She's alive?

The nurse laughed. Yes, she said. Because of you.

Me?

You kept her from bleeding to death.

It took me a while to process that. I saved Julia's life. Wow.

What's her blood type? I asked.

Blood type? What do you want to know that for?

Just indulge me, I said.

I can't tell you that, she said.

You've told me a lot already.

She bit her lip, doubtful. I don't know, she said.

Come on, I said. Did you know she works as a phlebotomist? She wouldn't care if I knew her blood type.

She never told me, though. Professional integrity or something like that.

As soon as the sedatives wore off enough I went down the hall to Julia's room. She looked pretty roughed up, like she had been through an ordeal.

She seemed to welcome me, even though there were other people in her room. Real relatives. Julia had a life. Not like me. They looked at me suspiciously until Julia told them I had helped her on the scene. Then they gathered around me and clapped me on the back and said thank you. I think I heard a hundred thank-yous that afternoon. Then I sat beside Julia and took her hand.

I'm sorry I wasn't able to give you blood, I said.

She shook her head. Don't be sorry, she said. I'm only glad you're okay.

On the television, there were reports of the children who had been killed at the school. I didn't want to hear the number. It was too awful. Julia and I held hands for a long time, each on the verge of tears.

I hate them, I said. I didn't tell her who I meant. I didn't tell her if it was the protesters, the cops, or the people who shot up the school.

I do too, she said.

And squeezed my hand.

Property Lines

Trevor's bee hives, twelve of them, sat like a boxy wooden mountain range on the horizon, just visible through my kitchen window, maybe a quarter mile distant. On still summer nights the buzz from their inhabitants wafted over my land and purred onto my ear drums. Not an unpleasant sound, but it reminded me how old I was that I didn't want to get up and go outside and stand by the hives.

I used to, when I was a little girl and first encountered bee hives. I loved the frenzied trembling of all those bustling insects. Loved how they made the air come alive. I knew they could sting, but they felt like friends to me. Made me think I might want to be a bee keeper when I grew up. It never happened. I worked for the county for four decades, clerking in the county courthouse, then retired to my golden years. Trevor brings me honey, sometimes. He calls me Mrs. Holding, which is fine, except that Mister Holding died more than twenty years ago and the name is beginning to acquire an awkward fit. I feel like I should have my own name now, not something that got put on me because I married a guy named Holding.

To me, Trevor is so polite you'd think he was a boy scout. But I know better. He thinks I'm batty. Maybe he's right. In town he calls me Old Lady Holding. Who talks that way? I've seen him draw a circle on his temple when he's talking about me. Well. That's all fine, too. Every town needs its batty old ladies. Without them, you don't have a proper town, now do you?

Just north of Trevor's hives, a little beyond a line of trees, stands Mary's old house, white and shiny against her perfectly manicured expansive lawn. Mary was a widow, like me. She used to be my friend until she took some of my land. That's what I said. Took. Stole. Whatever you want to call it. The worst part is she did it legally.

She didn't see what she did as theft, which is her privilege, I suppose, but the truth of the matter is that I had some land, then she did some legal hocus-pocus and then I didn't have that land anymore. Came to almost an acre and a half. Which left me with about twenty. Plenty for one old widow, but still. It grated on me what she did. Could be that she's why I'm still alive. I wanted her to die first. Seems only fair.

She was pretty healthy, though, so it wasn't a sure thing by any means. Except she did have a neurological issue. After a stroke a few years ago, the poor woman was prone to seizures. Not enough to kill her, but it did make her weaker. Not that I felt sorry for her. Nope. She could have dropped dead at any time and that would have been fine with me. She got the better share of the land, so I should get the better share of life. That make sense to you? It does to me.

How her crime took place hardly bears discussion anymore. I had some fruit trees—pears, apples, cherries—in a nice little corner of my property. I was even nice about the fruit. I let other people have them. Trevor and Mary, especially, since the corner was wedged in between their two properties, with Trevor's bees on one side and Mary's house on the other. And Mary liked fruit and honey. Especially honey. She put it in her tea, baked it into pies, and, I was sure, sometimes just spooned it into her mouth, straight from the jar. She adored honey-sweetened pies, so my fruit went hand in glove right with that honey.

I was generous with my fruit. Not just to Trevor and Mary. I took some of the fruit to work and passed it around. If kids wanted to come raid the trees, I didn't care. Kids *love* raiding fruit trees. Who was I to deny them that singular childhood joy? They could have the fruit. There were too many to eat myself, and I wasn't interested in going into the business of selling them, so, hey, free fruit for all.

Then Mary got it into her head to do a survey of her land. She even asked me to help pay for it. Pay for it? Why? What was in it for me?

She said she thought maybe the property lines were not accurate and it would be to both of our benefits to make sure they were set right.

Oh, sure. Only the line was just a couple of feet on the other side of my modest little grove. If the line moved my way it would take my trees away from me. If it moved her way, then I would get some more grass, which I really didn't need. I told her no thanks. If she thought something was wrong, then she would have to pay for it herself.

I'm sure if you asked Mary, she would have said our feud started then, when I refused to cooperate with her on finding out the TRUTH. But that's Mary. My position is that everything was fine with everyone until she started calculating how much money she could make from the fruit trees if she was able to sell all that fruit to the packers down by the river.

So the surveyors came out, with their *instruments* and their orange jackets and their tall poles marked off with tape. I half hoped that Trevor's bees would go for that bright orange and sting them to death.

Didn't happen. They went about their work for an afternoon and then they were gone. Well, a month later they delivered their report to Mary who immediately *came knocking at my door* to tell me, that, hey, who'd a thunk it, but the line between our properties was *not* what we thought it was all these years and it turns out the beautiful fruit trees were, in fact, on *her* property, and wow oh wow, isn't that just an amazing thing, huh, isn't it? Such redrawing of property lines is not unheard of in our area. Mistakes occur, and when the land was platted a hundred years ago, surveying techniques were sometimes applied in a slipshod fashion and often had to be corrected in subsequent years. I understood that, but here it was not *necessary*. She didn't *need* that extra slice of land.

Mary showed me the report with its official looking seal at the top and a nicely drawn map and a statement of legality or something. Does it matter? Mary had deftly brought to bear the forces of society in its petty attention to irrelevant detail and contrived, cleanly and brutally, to take my fruit trees from me. That which was large and strong and anchored in the ground was no match for her small-minded ways.

She tried to soften it. In her Mary way. She *thanked* me for taking care of the trees for as long as I had been doing it. She was so *grateful* at the wonderful job I had done.

Taking care of them? I *planted* the bloody things almost fifty years ago. They were *mine*. Or the Earth's. Certainly not Mary's. They were never Mary's trees. No.

She also said I could take as much fruit from them as I wanted. Within reason. She didn't mind, but that I had to remember not to take *too* many since she was going to be selling them and didn't want to lose *too* much money on the deal and she was sure I would understand. Also, would it be too much bother if I would make sure the local young folks who liked to come raid the trees would stay off her property from now on? In fact, it would be best for the whole neighborhood if I just made it known that I didn't abide trespassers on my property, period, since the only reason to come on my land now was to gain access to *her* land and the trees. The fruit. Her fruit.

Yes, you could say that Mary had a lot of nerve. It served her well but didn't do much for me.

I told Mary I would see what I could do but she knew and I knew that I had no intention of policing the neighborhood so her fruit would be safe from raiders. But she didn't press the point. Not then, anyway.

After she left I sat in my kitchen and looked out at the trees. I could no longer say *my* trees and that hurt more than I can say.

Trevor came over later in the afternoon with a couple of jars of honey.

I opened the door for him, but I wasn't in a talking mood.

"Hi Mrs. Holding," he said. "What's up at Mary's place?"

"Probably planning a campaign to steal your bees," I said.

"What?" He looked at me like I was bonkers. Loony tunes.

"Never mind," I said. "What have you got for me today?"

"Honey," he said with a big grin on his face as he thrust two big jars toward me. "The bees have been busy, you know? I like to spread the bounty."

I took the jars, but still didn't let him in. He saw that I was being reticent, so he didn't press it. "Looks like a fence," he said.

"What?"

"Mary. Looks like she's building a fence." He gestured with a motion of his head. I followed the indicated direction and saw a couple of burly guys Mary must have hired using post diggers to sink holes into my land. Which was now Mary's land. Well. She worked fast, did Mary.

"We had a transfer of property," I said.

Trevor scratched his head. "If you say so Mrs. Holding."

"I do say so," I said.

"Well, enjoy the honey." He touched his forehead. I half expected him to draw that circle on his temple, but he didn't.

"Trevor?" I said.

"Yes Mrs. Holding."

"You still take honey to Mary?"

"Why sure I do," he said. "Like I tell everyone, the bees are good to me. I like to spread my luck. Mary loves my honey. She'd eat it every meal if she could."

I nodded, adopting as dark a demeanor as I could muster. I think it must have worked, because he looked about as nervous as I've ever seen him. I think I might have put the fear in him, which made me feel good.

Over the next couple of days I watched the fence go up, post by post, then plank by plank, and as each piece of it obscured more and more of my grove—excuse me, *her* grove—I felt my blood boil. I didn't want to see an ugly old fence staring back across from me whenever I looked across my land. So I figured I'd plant something in front of it. Some fruit trees would be nice, but they weren't going to grow fast enough. I'd probably be dead, or nearly so, before they ever bore fruit. Instead, I looked through some of my catalogs and came across an interesting New Zealand shrub called tutu with some attractive properties that suited my mood. For one thing, it was thick. For another, it grew fast. It also had pretty flowers. I liked that. I ordered some and they arrived soon after and I had Trevor dig holes along Mary's fence and plant them for me.

They looked good. A natural row of shrubbery is better than a wooden fence. I walked up to them and strolled along their stately rows. The summer was almost over. A slight chill in the air let me know fall was coming. Trevor's hives, a short distance away, still buzzed and rustled the air, but more subdued, like sleep had overtaken them. I looked across Mary's fence to the fruit trees. They were mostly bare. The leaves had fallen away. The apples and pears had been picked already. Next season all those blossoms that arrive in spring would be for Mary. Trevor's bees would crawl over them and make honey from the sap they collected, just like they had for years, only the honey would be different. I know it hardly makes any sense to say it because the blossoms don't know which side of a fence they are on, but I knew the nectar they would yield would make the honey bitter on my tongue.

I walked closer to Trevor's hives. Even though the bees were quieter, I still wanted to be near them. They felt like kindred spirits to me: older and quieter, perhaps, but retaining the sting of life in them. I knew they were as potent as they had ever been.

Winter was particularly cold and snowy that year. White fluffy flakes seemed to fall on a daily basis. Before the middle of January, it had piled up to ten feet in some places. I was happy to see, though, that my tutu shrubs did just fine. In fact, they seemed to thrive and when spring came and they blossomed with amazing rows of bright white flowers, Trevor's bees woke up and drank in their nectar like it was going out of style. Later in the spring Mary's fruit trees blossomed and the bees did their dance on those flowers, but it wasn't the same. Didn't have the same power to move me.

When I went to town to do my shopping and my banking, I told everyone I met that Mary was in charge of my grove of trees now, and that she welcomed anyone coming over and helping themselves to the fruit. Just like I did when I was in charge of them. This news met with approval, especially from the young folks. "Thanks, Mrs. Holding," they said.

"You're so welcome," I told them, and I smiled. Beamed.

I remember that summer as a pleasant buzz of sun and bees. As one gets older, the sun becomes more and more of a friend, the way it keeps away the cold. My bones never took to cold very well. They welcomed the enveloping heat, the soft intensity of sunlight wrapping my body.

Mary came over one August evening. I saw her coming.

I opened the door to her after letting her knock for a long time.

"Yes, Mary," I said.

"You've been telling people they can eat my fruit," she said.

"Well, I didn't think you'd mind," I said.

Her mouth was set very firm, like she could crack a nut if you set one between her lips. "That's *not* what I told you," she said.

"Well," I said, "I was sure you would reconsider. There's a long standing tradition with those trees, you know. It's all about precedent, isn't it? The precedent of free access. You don't just cut that off without warning. Think of it as an easement. Easements have tradition behind them. Tradition is good, right? Aren't you going to make traditional apple pies from all those apples on your property now?"

"You *know* I want those apples and those pears and those cherries to *sell*. You *know* that. I *told* you that. I need the income. I'm a poor widow."

Poor widow my ass. Mary's just greedy. "Share, Mary," I said. "Don't you know it's good to share?"

"Stop telling people they can have my fruit. I'll call the police on you."

The police. I was shaking in my slippers.

"Is that all?" I said.

She started to say something else, probably to call me a name, but she held her tongue. She was turning so red I half expected her to have a convulsion or a seizure right there on my front step. But she didn't. She turned and walked away. That was the last time I saw her.

Trevor came over with that blasted honey of his again. I tried not to show my impatience.

"Those bushes you had me plant," he said. "My bees love them. Must have a lot of nectar in them. They made so much honey, I have to give away twice as much as usual."

"Oh, Trevor," I said. "That's awfully nice of you, but I still have some of your honey from last year. Why don't you take those jars to Mary. I know she loves your honey."

He scratched his head. "You sure about that Mrs. Holding?" he said. "Aren't you two in a big fight right now?"

"Whatever gave you that idea?" I said.

"Everyone's talking about it. They say she's mad at you and you're mad at her. All about those fruit trees."

I saw the light in his eyes. He enjoyed the thought of a good old fashioned feud in his back yard. Even if the feuders are a couple of old widows. I understood the impulse. I was not immune to the entertainment value of such things. But nevertheless, I sought to downplay my part in the spectacle.

"Mary has her issues," I said. "You know she has medical problems. They can make her head screwy." I twirled my index finger around my temple.

He had the grace to turn slightly red. His ears at least. "I didn't know that," he said.

I nodded vigorously. "Oh yes," I said. "She's battier than me by a long shot." I smiled. "Ask anyone."

"I'll do that, Mrs. Holding," he said, obviously done with me. Maybe unnerved by me. He took a couple of small steps backwards, those giant jars of honey tucked under his arms. I half expected him to drop them to the ground. But he didn't. I waved at him and he turned and walked toward Mary's house.

Oh, Mary and her honey. Back when we were still friends I observed her honey-fiend ways. She would invite me over for some tea and she'd drip honey into her cup, smear it on an English muffin, and lick her fingers, getting every last drop. I saw how much it meant to her. Saw the love in her eyes. The craving for it.

I was only too pleased to make her happy.

But, alas, her life took a tragic turn. That fall, just before Halloween, after she had harvested her fruit and sold them to the packers, while she was busy making pumpkin pies in her kitchen (laced with generous amounts of Trevor's honey) she keeled over onto the floor, in a stone cold coma.

I didn't learn about it right away. It was a couple of days. Halloween, in fact, when some kids came trick-or-treating and they told me they had been at Mary's house and no one answered the door when they knocked. I said "Maybe she's turned into a ghost for Halloween," and they laughed, but I was dead serious.

Later that night I went over to her house and found her on the kitchen floor. A jar of honey, now covered with ants, lay broken by her side. I put my hand on her neck. There was a faint pulse. I sighed and went to her phone and called the ambulance.

They got there quick, but she had been in her coma for too long. They took her to the hospital and she died a couple of days later. At her memorial I delivered a heart-felt eulogy, asking her forgiveness for my part in our feud. I was half moved by my own words, and I know my fellow citizens completely approved of what I said. Thought the batty old lady had seen the light.

Mary's property went up for sale soon after that. It sold quickly and the new owners and me get along just fine. I told them all about the history of the land and the fruit trees, and wouldn't you know it, I lucked out and got some very nice neighbors indeed. They said they didn't want any fence and they'd be happy to take it out and I could take all the fruit I wanted and spend all the time with my trees that I wanted to. They *liked* having a little old lady puttering around the property.

Well.

I thanked them and got Trevor to come pull up the shrubs he had put it only a couple of years before that. I stood next to the hives as he worked, listening to the bees buzz. Oh, my, but the sound of them, their scurrying and bustling, it settled me right down.

When Trevor finished, after he had loaded up all those shrubs on the back of his truck and tied them in preparation for taking them to the county chipper, he came up to me and said, "All done, Mrs. Holding."

"Thank you, Trevor," I said.

"Those trees look a lot better without all that fencing and shrubbery hemming them in."

"Don't they?" I said.

"Good thing we took that shrubbery out anyway," he said.

"Oh?"

"Yeah. I was doing some reading and that particular shrub, that tutu plant, when bees get into the flowers, they make a certain chemical in the honey. Well, this book where I read about it, it says it can make the honey poisonous. Creates some kind of chemical that puts people in comas."

As he spoke, I barely heard his words. I was concentrating on the bees. The way the noise of them wrapped itself around my eardrums and gave me a kind of gooey feeling, like I was curled up on the couch with a good hot cup of tea.

"Is that right, Trevor?" I said. "My, that is truly frightening. Who'd have ever thought such a thing was even possible?"

This Sudden Execution of My Will

THE EXECUTIONER SLID the shiny silver blade under the flap and burst the fold with a quick, practiced stroke. He set the letter opener down on the kitchen table and upended the envelope. Several large denomination bills spilled out onto the table like unwinding entrails.

He grunted.

"What is it, Dear?"

The executioner looked up from the morning mail. Helen, his wife, sat quietly in her chair, reading the latest *People* magazine.

"Money," said the executioner.

"Really?" said Helen. "Who's sending us money?" She put the magazine down on her lap. It was open to a story about an actor who had recently killed himself.

"I don't know," said the executioner. He held the envelope up to the light over the table. "No postmark, no return address, nothing. Where do you suppose it came from?"

"Who cares. How much?"

He counted it out. "Five hundred and fifty dollars," he said.

Helen whistled. "Someone must really like us. What should we use it for? A new TV would be nice. And you could use some clothes—those awful T-shirts you wear are terrible."

The executioner listened carefully. He would like some new things too, but he did not like this free money. It made him feel peculiar in the pit of his stomach, like something was not right with the universe. He had the notion that someone was watching him, studying him, waiting for him to—what? He did not know, but it made him uneasy.

"I think," said the executioner, "that maybe we shouldn't spend it just yet."

Helen sighed. "I might have known you'd get guilty about something like this. Can't you just take the money and run?"

The executioner arranged the bills into a neat pile and stuffed them into his pocket. He went to Helen and kissed her. "It bothers me to get this money like this. I need to know where it's coming from."

She sighed again. "What are you going to do?"

The *People* slid from her lap onto the floor. He pointed at it. "Your magazine," he said.

"What are you going to do about the money?" said Helen.

"I don't know," he said.

THE WOMAN AT the post office was not interested in the executioner's problem. "I don't think I can help you," she said.

"I really need to know where this envelope came from," said the executioner.

"I told you I don't know," said the woman. "Without a postmark or return address there's no way I can tell."

"Well someone here must have put it in my box."

She shrugged. "Marilyn worked this morning, but I'm telling you she won't know either."

"You know something," said the executioner. "You know what's going on."

"I'm sure I don't know what you're talking about. Do you need anything else?"

He asked for some stamps and she put them into a small translucent envelope for him.

"Thanks," he said and tossed some money onto the counter.

Outside the post office the air was cool and fresh. He wondered what he had expected to discover by coming here. Of course there was no way they would be able to tell him where the letter had come from. They got thousands of letters everyday coming through the post office, it was not possible to know where each one had come from.

He stepped out to his car and sat in the driver's seat for many minutes, waiting for something to tell him what to do next. The money was still a strange bulge in his pocket, annoying him, clamoring for his attention.

He fingered the crackling envelope the clerk had given him. It was shiny like waxed paper. The stamps inside looked like they were under a blurry pool of water. He took a row of them out and examined them carefully. They had a picture of the president on them, with the words "US Postage 33" along the side. Huh. That wasn't the current postage rate. Why would the clerk sell him these old stamps? Then a shot of adrenalin went through him and he sat up quickly. He got out of the car and ran back to the post office.

A different clerk stood behind the counter. He looked up and smiled as the executioner approached. "What can I do for you?"

"These stamps," said the executioner. "These stamps are wrong. There's something wrong with them."

The clerk maintained a pleasant demeanor but the executioner could tell he was suspicious. "Let me see them."

The executioner stepped back. "No. Let me see the woman that sold them to me."

"I don't know who sold them to you, sir. If you'd let me look at them, I'd be able to help you."

"I was just here five minutes ago. The clerk was a woman. Let me talk to her. I want to talk to her."

Now the clerk looked puzzled. "But I've been here since we opened this morning."

The executioner felt the presence of people behind him in line, silently urging him to get out of the way.

"You don't understand," he said. "These stamps have a picture of a *live* person on them. The only portraits allowed on stamps are dead people. You know that. Everyone knows that. It's a post office *rule*. Hell, it's probably a federal *law*." He clutched the envelope with the stamps and held his hand close to his chest. The clerk now looked bewildered. He clearly wanted the executioner gone.

Someone brushed past the executioner and approached the clerk. Murmurs came from some of the other people in line. He did not quite understand what they were saying but he heard words like "crazy" and "nutso." He stepped back and the line flowed past him. The clerk avoided his gaze and instead concentrated on his new customers. The executioner went out into the fresh air again. He knew he was right. These stamps did not make sense. They could not have been printed by the post office.

HELEN WAS ABSORBED by the daily paper when the executioner returned home. There was a juicy story about a lurid murder in the adjoining county. She barely looked up at him. "We got an email," she said. "From your mother. Your father died."

The executioner stopped in the middle of removing his jacket. He became aware of his heart beat. The only other sound in the room was the rustling of the newspaper in Helen's hand. "My father," he said.

"Yes. Terrible accident, it sounds like. Some farm machinery thing."

His father still lived in the old country, on the farm where he was born, the farm he still worked at the age of seventy. Or used to work. The executioner went to the laptop and read the email. It was just as Helen had said.

"Interesting story about that poor Everly girl," said Helen. "Do you know they found her with her insides all scrambled up? Someone had taken out her organs and then put them back every which way. What kind of person could do such a thing?" She shook her head and sighed.

The executioner sat down and put his arms on the kitchen table.

"Helen," he said quietly.

"What is it, dear?"

"My father's dead."

"I know that, dear. I just told you."

"I'm scared."

"No, you're in shock. There's a difference. That'll pass, to be replaced by grief. A horrible sadness. After that, well, it depends on who you are as a person. What kind of grit you have. You could fall into a depression, or you could rally your strength and become a better human being. I'm willing to bet on the better human being. Always best to believe in the positive, don't you think?"

Was Helen really telling him about how he felt? And how he was going to feel?

"Okay," he said. "I'm in shock. I think." He wasn't at all sure what he was experiencing. His gut felt like something had been ripped out of it. His spine would not stop tingling, as if something was crawling up and down it continuously, something he didn't want to know about.

"Now don't worry," said Helen. "Just put it out of your mind. That's what I do. When my sister died last year you didn't see me making a fuss, did you? Of course not. Your father was old, time for him to go anyway. Plus, he worked too hard and didn't take care of himself. It's a wonder he didn't die sooner. It's better this way." Helen twisted around in her chair to look at the executioner and smiled at him.

He tried to smile back but he could not make the muscles in his face do as he wished.

"My poor, sad, dear," said Helen and turned back to her newspaper.

The executioner pulled out the translucent envelope with the stamps bearing the picture of the living president. Ever since he received the money that morning things were not as they should be. Helen suddenly becoming numb to death. The clerk at the post office disappearing into thin air. The stamps. These crazy stamps.

He cleared his throat and rose from the chair. He went to the kitchen drawer and pulled out a pad of paper, some envelopes, and a pen. He sat back down at his chair and adjusted the paper in front of him.

"I'm going to write a letter and find out about this money," he said.

"That's nice," said Helen. "Here's a story on page ten of the Living section about a terrible accident on the interstate. Five people dead. Now why do you suppose they'd bury something this good way back in the paper like that?"

The executioner didn't answer. Helen folded back the paper and settled in to read the story.

The executioner pulled off the top sheet and wrote the following in big letters: "WHO IS SENDING ME MONEY?" Then he folded up the paper into thirds and put it in the envelope. He sealed the envelope and printed his return address in the corner. He wrote "TO WHOM IT MAY CONCERN" across the front of the envelope. Finally, he took one of the living president stamps and stuck it in the top right corner. He did not recall ever doing anything like this, and yet he knew it was the proper thing to do. Whoever knew about the money would find his message and get back to him.

"I'm going to the post office again," he said to Helen.

She was leafing through the rest of the paper. "Fine, dear," she said. "Take your time."

HE FOUND THE original clerk at the post office. He smiled at her as he walked up to her window. "I loved those stamps you sold me," he said.

She did not smile back. "Okay," she said.

"Here's a letter I need to mail. I'm sure you know what to do with it."

She took the envelope from him and examined the face of it.

"Everything looks fine," she said.

The executioner chuckled. "I'm sure it does. Well, bye." She nodded at him and he saw that she did not throw the letter in with the rest of the mail, but instead set it off to one side, no doubt to be sure it got the special treatment it needed.

WHEN HE RETURNED home Helen was still in the same place, facing away from him, but the newspaper she had been devouring lay in tatters all over the living room floor.

He felt irritated with her. "You don't have to make a mess," he said.

"I finished it," she said. "Now it's your turn."

That was not Helen's voice. It was deeper, slower, more mellow, like the sound of a voice coming from a cavern. A bolt of fear cut through the executioner. Helen turned around. Her face was different; not Helen's face at all. She looked like an older, more life-battered version of the clerk at the post office.

The executioner stepped back and felt the wall of his house press against his spine. He felt his heart rattling in his chest. His head was dizzy.

"I said," said Helen who was not Helen, "it's your turn again." She stood up and walked toward him. She seemed taller than the Helen he had known all these years, like she had been stretched and pulled. Her arms moved in slow graceful arcs as she talked. Her hair flowed behind her like tentacles underwater. The executioner sank to the floor, absolutely powerless under the force of this person and his own fear.

"Don't you remember?" said Helen.

The executioner looked up. Helen's nostrils hung over him like two black eyes at the top of a tall monster.

"Remember what?" said the executioner finally.

An expression of wonderment seemed to cross Helen's face. "You don't remember," she said in amazement.

The executioner trembled with fear.

"How could you remember the stamp and message, but forget all the rest?"

The executioner did not answer.

"Well, no matter," said Helen. "I suppose I should go over the whole thing again with you, but I'm really not in the mood. Here's the way it is. We need an executioner. None of our people will do the job. Morals and all, you know. Yet we have these criminals who need to die. What to do, what to do? A real dilemma, huh? But a solution presents itself in the form of interdimensional travel. I believe that's what you would call it. We make life hell for you in this dimension and agree to fix everything on one condition: that you become the executioner for our dimension. Is it clear?"

The executioner trembled. His teeth began chattering. He felt so cold, so alone, so lonely. What had happened to his Helen, to his world?

"Well, I suppose it isn't all that clear, is it? No matter. Let's get done with this." She put a cardboard box in front of the executioner. He stared at it. "Open it," she said. He did so. Inside was a crystalline object about the size of a baseball. "Now then, here's the deal. You crumble this ball and your world is back the way you want it, and, not incidentally, our criminal is dispatched forthwith. You don't crumble the ball and your life remains like it has been for the past few hours. Your choice. What'll it be?"

The executioner looked at Helen's eyes. There was fire behind them, the light of another world? Maybe. He looked through the window. The colors of the trees and sky slid into one another like globs of paint. The house was dark and drooping. It seemed to be collapsing around him, and the ceiling was sagging and soggy, like a pouch filled with dripping entrails.

The executioner took the ball in his hand. He felt Helen's gaze on him. This new Helen, whatever she was. She did not think of him as a person, but rather an unimportant animal who could be prodded and tortured into doing her tasks for her. A slave. A beast unfit for anything but killing.

The ball was hot and cold and soft and hard. He covered it with both his hands and applied pressure. It seemed to give, and as it did Helen seemed to diminish in size. Her hair stopped flowing. The executioner pressed harder. The ceiling returned to its original flat shape. The colors outside corrected themselves and stopped flowing into one another. He pressed again, harder, as though giving his last burst of strength. A pain shot through his body, from his feet to his head.

He screamed. Helen gasped.

Somewhere, he knew, a being died. Another execution had been performed. He opened his hands. The ball was nothing but a handful of dust. He slapped his palms together and looked up. Helen was not in front of him any longer. He looked around wildly. There was no email from his mother on the laptop. Nothing to indicate his father had died. He knew, deep in the pit of his gut, that in fact his father *hadn't* died. Relief washed over him.

"Where's the email?" he asked Helen

"What email?" she said.

"From my mother."

"Your mother doesn't send emails, for goodness sake. Where did you get an idea like that? Are you all right dear?"

Helen sat on the couch. Her newspaper was open to the comics page. She looked concerned.

Yes, thought the executioner, everything was back to normal. It was over again. All he had to do now was forget about it. Put it out of his mind. There were ways to do that. Ways to make his life sane again until the next time. All it took was mental power. The need to have everything normal again was the most powerful force he knew.

He stood up and smiled crookedly. "I'm fine," he said. "How about us going out and spending our windfall?"

Helen jumped up and clapped her hands. "I thought you'd never ask."

Parallel Moons

1a

I NEVER UNDERSTOOD the term "new moon." When the moon is invisible, how can it be new? "New moon" should be called "empty moon," the opposite of full moon. I resolved to use the term when I was quite young. I figured all my friends would agree with me and we'd start a new way of talking about the moon. Only thing is, the phases of the moon don't come up in conversation all that often, so the terminology never caught on.

Another thing I remember about the moon: I used to put my finger over it to make it disappear. Lots of kids did that. There's immense power in erasing an object big enough to have its own gravity. Kids crave that kind of power. They want to rule the world.

2a

YOU WORK AT a medium-sized law firm. You get a call from some nerds. Space cadets. They want to reclassify the moon. They say it's a planet, not a satellite. You think this has to be some kind of joke. But no. They are dead serious. They have *money* to pay for your legal work. Seven hundred and eighty-six dollars. And thirty-two cents. They collected it by passing a hat.

You are amused. You take the case. Why not? No point in being who you are unless you can have some fun once in a while, right? Right?

3a

ALICE CREIGHTON KNEW as much about Richard Mollene as anyone who ever looked at a gossip website, which made sense, since she wrote for one of the most popular. Mollene was the richest person ever, a complete recluse, a widower, and dedicated to three things above all else: stopping global warming, halting disease, and making the moon disappear. He had already accomplished the first with his innovative solar cell technology, had made real progress on the second with his universal vaccine, and now, with the pepper mill in orbit around the moon for the past twenty years, he was well on his way to achieving the third.

Alice approved of Mollene's first two dreams, but was not in favor of the third. A lot of people said they understood Richard Mollene and his pepper mill.

Alice Creighton did not. She asked for an interview with Mollene to get more information. To her surprise, he said yes. Alice would get face time with the man who set the pepper mill grinding and seasoning the moon from lunar orbit two decades ago. A lot of people said its mission was impossible. They said fine non-reflective dust, no matter how abundant, couldn't quench the light of the moon.

But they were wrong.

1b

LIKE MOST EVERYONE else, I saw the alien craft arrive on the moon via TV. Unlike most others, I did my watching from inside a correctional institution, the state prison. Don't feel sorry for me. I had embezzled a lot of money and I got caught, fair and square. I was paying my debt to society.

There wasn't a lot of fuss when the aliens arrived. It was during a full moon. One minute they weren't there. The next, spaceships were landing on lunar craters and mountains. Astronomers everywhere had been tracking the ships for months, so we knew they were coming.

People were insulted at first. The aliens saw fit to go to the moon, but none of them bothered to visit the dominant species on Earth? It was as though humans did not count in the eyes of the aliens. After thinking about this for a while, people stopped being insulted and began to worry.

Over the next few days it became obvious that there were no aliens. The spaceships contained terraforming machines. They crawled out of the ships and immediately set to work transforming the moon into a livable planet with vegetation, an atmosphere, and water.

No nation had the resources or the guts to send a crew to the moon to investigate. We had to watch from afar, with telescopes, a set of circumstances which disgusted many, including me. Fact is, we should have been right there, on the moon, either observing the process or putting a stop to it.

2b

YOU LISTEN AS the nerds tell you about *the* footprint. The one left by Neil Armstrong when he first stepped off the LEM decades and decades ago. They want to preserve the footprint. Neil Armstrong is dead and gone. People have not been to the moon in decades. The footprint, *the* footprint, (actually a boot print, if you really want to be accurate) would not last much longer. All the constant heating and cooling of the lunar soil that bears the image of the print, constantly expanding and contracting, loosening and settling, was altering the print. The nerds tell you that even now it is probably already more blurred than sharp. There is little time to waste if the print is to be preserved.

The nerds show you a plan that will dig up the print without disturbing it and bring it back *intact* to the Earth. To be put up in a museum, no doubt, maybe the Air and Space in Washington DC. The print will inspire a new generation of space explorers, that's what the nerds say. But to do that we have to *go* to the moon. Except no one wants to do that anymore. If they go anywhere, it will be to Mars. Mars is where it's at. Mars is a *planet*. The moon is, well, a moon. Nothing but a lowly satellite.

But you can change that.

3b

ALICE TRIED TO find the moon in the sky. Her almanac told her it was full, but it took a while for her to find it, barely visible and high in the sky. The pepper mill had done its job admirably. About the only people who were happy about the moon slowly slipping from view were the astronomers. They never did like the moon's glare, the way it splashed light all over the sky. Made observing the stars tough. Damn near impossible sometimes.

But the rest of humanity? The lovers, the dreamers, the werewolves, the eclipse watchers, all who appreciated and hungered for beauty, what about them? They missed the moon. Alice missed the moon. She wanted it back. She was going to go to the source, to the man who built the mill and set it grinding, to find out one thing: *why?*

3a

MY GRANDFATHER WORKED on the original Apollo project, the one that put *people* on the moon and brought them back to Earth. Twelve of them. All dead now, more than sixty years after the last one came home and we have not been back since. Not just Americans. *No one* from *any* country has gone back safely.

I could only imagine what kind of machinations were going on behind the scenes at NASA and the oval office over alien terraforming machines on the moon.

A few months after it started, astronomers reported a new development: comets were coming our way. Hundreds of them. At first we thought they were on a collision course for Earth. Mild panic for a few days. Until they figured out the comets were going to the moon instead. Speculation ran rampant. The best guess was that the alien terraformers wanted water on the moon. The best way to do that was to crash a bunch of comets on the surface. The moon would get billions of tons of water in no time since comets are mostly ice.

So we waited and watched. We wondered what alien power could tip all those comets from the Oort Cloud to come raining down on the moon. Again, much speculation, but nothing concrete. The aliens, if indeed that is who was responsible, never showed themselves. Not once.

The comets arrived. None of them crashed into the moon, much to the disappointment of billions of tv viewers. Instead the comets took up orbits around the moon. Long eccentric orbits. Some experts saw what was happening immediately. The moon was *receding* from the Earth under the influence of the pulling forces of the comets. The retreat was slow, but steady. The damned aliens were not only developing *our* only natural satellite for their own purposes, they were *stealing* it right from under us.

I was incensed, but I was in the minority.

I wrote letters to the president. Lots of them. I said we had to do something. Anything. We had to stop this theft.

Most people, though, simply did not care. The astronomers, especially. They said the moon interfered with their observations anyway, throwing all that light on the night sky. If the moon was gone, they could get a lot more work done.

I have to say, I never thought of that.

3b

SO THE NERDS tell you the only way to go to the moon is to convince people it is not a moon at all but a twin planet of the Earth. And for that they need you. A lawyer. They are petitioning the International Astronomical Union to have the moon declared a sister planet of the Earth. There are precedents, they tell you. Pluto was reclassified. Also, if the Earth and moon were discovered in another solar system today, they would be considered twin planets because of the size of the moon relative to the Earth. It is only fair and right to make them twin planets here.

So earnest, these nerds. So intent on that boot print. They amuse you with their belief that fair and right matter.

You tell them their idea makes no sense. Changing the name of something does not change the thing. They tell you that you are wrong. All disputes are about semantics, they say. They have linguists to back them up on this. Philosophers and experts on cognitive concepts. Semantics is destiny, the nerds tell you. More than once.

You think they are crazy, but you don't tell them this. You are still entertained by them.

You start to research this classification business. Much of it is arbitrary. There is no real ironclad definition for what a planet is. So that leaves wiggle room. The moon really could be called a planet. It makes sense. Suddenly you begin to see the wisdom of the nerds. They make a lot of sense. You are fired up by the challenge. You pelt the IAU with petitions for reclassification of the moon. They ignore all of your efforts.

This does not discourage you. On the contrary, you begin to sense a challenge. You redouble your efforts. You research all cases of classification revisions of the past. You find a way in. You tell the nerds they need to find a group of astronomers, prominent in the field, who will go along with their scheme. With that kind of back up, you can make some progress.

The nerds listen very carefully.

3c

ALICE WAS AWARE most people thought of Richard Mollene as a kind of mad man. A rich mad man who made his fortune immorally. He was also a sad lover who decided he couldn't stand looking at the moon. It reminded him of his wife, Sally, who loved the moon, but who had died early in their marriage. Terribly sad story, romantic and beautiful.

And Alice never believed a word of it.

Now, she hoped, she was about to find out the real story.

Alice arrived at Mollene's house around midnight. He always

received visitors late at night. Was there something about simply *having* that much money that made people eccentric? Maybe. Alice shouldered her camera bag and greeted the guard at the gate. He checked over his logbook and asked for Alice's bag.

"I need it for my interview," she said.

"Sorry, no cameras, tape recorders, camcorders, or senscorders."

"But—"

"Those are the rules. You don't have to go in if you don't want to."

"They're one of *his* senscorders."

"He doesn't want them in the house."

An inventor who didn't want his own invention near him? More eccentricity. Alice sighed and handed over the bag.

"It'll be waiting here when you leave," said the guard.

"How about a pad and pencil?" said Alice.

"No."

The guard punched a button and a gate swung open. Alice walked down a paved path toward a building that would have glowed like a haunted house in the moonlight not two decades ago. The front door swung open as she approached it.

A man in formal clothes greeted her and took her coat. He showed her to a lushly furnished room lined with bookshelves. Mr. Mollene would join her in a few minutes.

4a

ANOTHER THING I had not thought about was the tides. What with climate change and all, a lot of coastal areas were getting flooded. High tides tended to make things even worse. Without the moon— no tides! People could hang onto their seaside property that much longer.

Well, okay. I saw the benefit of that.

But it didn't matter. I still wanted the moon to stay up in the sky. Was that too much to ask?

My cell mate didn't care. "I'm in jail," he said. "What do I care about the moon?"

"We're not going to be here forever," I said. "Don't you want to see the moon in the sky when you get out?"

"Because it's romantic?"

"Something like that."

"No. I don't care."

Prison can do that to a person. Make you apathetic. I wasn't apathetic. I was the opposite. I was completely obsessed with this one issue. The moon. Prison can do that to you too.

So here's the picture: The moon was being overrun by cosmic developers turning it from a pretty cool dead cinder into some kind of suburbia for intergalactic somethings. And, in addition, it was being towed away by the gravitational effects of orbiting comets. And, oh yeah, one other thing: the people of Earth couldn't do a damned thing about it.

4b

THE NERDS THANK you for the suggestion. They go out and begin their search. You want to help them, you really do. You see the historical significance of the print. You want that print back on Earth. You seem to be turning into a nerd yourself.

The nerds come back. Very excited. They tell you they have assembled a team of astronomers. Lots of them. They all agree that the moon is not a moon. It is a planet.

You are thrilled. With such a team, there is no doubt you can present a formidable case. You begin to draw up a new petition. You are *into* this. You spend several hours with the nerds as they help you with language and fine points. The committee wants things a certain way, you see, and only the nerds can help you there.

The nerds tell you that they are working for the betterment of humanity. We need a dream, they say. The print will reawaken the dream of space travel.

You tell the nerds they are inspiring. You continue the work, long since having put it in the category of pro bono cases. You begin to neglect your other clients. You don't care. You practice your delivery to the committee in front of a mirror for hours on end.

The committee sends word: They will hear your case. You and the nerds appear before the committee and you launch into your spiel. The committee members listen politely. You are on fire, bringing in scientific precedent, the testimony of living scientists, and good old common sense. You lay out the reasoning with devastating logic. You know you have nailed the case. You have to win.

The committee says it needs to consider the case and will issue a ruling in two weeks.

4c

THE BUTLER RETREATED from the room and left Alice to her own devices. She'd never been in a rich person's house before, not rich like this anyway. Mollene had more money than the queen—than all queens combined, probably. He was the only private person on the planet with the funds to send up his own rocket to the moon. Actually, a succession of rockets, hundreds of them, each one sending blankets of "pepper" to the moon's surface.

Alice sat for a while, then got fidgety. She went to the bookshelves. Lots of trashy bestsellers, a few picture books. Did Mollene have them here because his guests often spent a lot of time waiting for him?

She leafed through magazines. Mollene apparently still liked getting them on paper. Another eccentricity, she supposed. She was starting to get a little drowsy when the door swung open and a small man who looked to be about eighty shuffled in on scratchy sounding slippers.

"Miss Creighton?" he said with a surprisingly solid voice. Alice had seen pictures of him, of course, but had never heard him speak. His eyes were dull, his skin was dry and wrinkled. He seemed tired, used up.

"Mr. Mollene," she said. "I'm glad to meet you." She rose and offered her hand. He shuffled by her and sat down on a chair. He pulled out a pack of cigarettes and lit one and took a long puff then blew the smoke up towards the ceiling. Mollene was a nicotine hound. Alice was surprised. No one had ever guessed that about him. Mollene looked at Alice but did not say a word.

Alice sensed it was up to her to get things going. "Why did you agree to this interview?" she said.

"You're the first one who's asked me in years."

"People gave up asking because they thought you never talked to the press."

"Well, they were wrong. I'm talking to you."

It had been at least ten years since Alice had known anyone who smoked. Her eyes stung from Mollene's cigarette smoke.

"Why did you take away the moon?" she said.

Mollene studied her for a few second. "The pepper mill isn't going to go on forever, you know."

"Sure I know. Everyone knows. After it has blotted out the moon, it'll stop."

"The moon," said Mollene. "Everyone cries for the moon like it's some poor lost soul. People really need to get over that."

5a

THEN THE BIGGEST surprise. They let me out early.

I had a couple of years left on my sentence. But one morning they came to my cell and told me I got some kind of pardon. From the president, no less. Guess my letters had an effect.

My cell mate looked at me like I was some kind of magician. I shrugged my shoulders, conveying to him that I had no idea what was going on.

They hustled me out of the prison before I could say boo. Two guys in suits. I asked them where I was going, because it didn't look like I was going home. They didn't say anything. They put me in a car, then put me on a plane. A really nice one.

The three of us were the only passengers.

They handed me a sheaf of papers. They told me I needed to read them. So I did.

Looked like I was to be part of a task force. We were to figure out what to do about the moon getting stolen. My expertise was required because I was a criminal. The good kind. I'm not kidding. The thinking was that a criminal mind, my kind of criminal mind, the kind that does not do violence, thinks effectively outside the box and knows how to cut through red tape and bureaucracies to get things done.

I asked my two escorts if this was for real.

They said nothing. I assumed they were supposed to say nothing.

They brought me food. I read through more of the papers. The task force had a big job ahead of it. At the current rate of acceleration the moon would be gone from the solar system in a few years. We would never see it again, except perhaps as a tiny dot lost among the stars.

5b

THE PRESS BESIEGES you. The case of the nerds has the world enthralled. Do they really think they can reclassify the moon? You wonder. As the days go on you begin to second guess yourself. Did you make the best argument? Did a good argument even matter? Was this all for naught? You are obsessed. Your employer tells you you look tired. She recommends you take a vacation. She quietly assigns your cases to other lawyers.

By the time the committee reconvenes, the press corps has become enormous. You and the nerds barely have room to fit into the hall. Flash bulbs pop all over the place. A general loud *presence*. Some of the committee members look frightened. They are not used to this much attention.

The first committee member speaks. He explicates his reasons for denying the petition. The nerds hoot at him. You tell them to shush, but they will not be silenced. Some of the nerds drop their pants and display their buttocks to the committee. You laugh, despite your horror at their antics. No client of yours ever does such things. Until now. Security removes the offenders from the room.

The remaining committee members each speak in turn. They give their own personal feelings on the pros and cons of the petition. You listen carefully, trying to catch the subtext of each speech. Soon you think you know how the decision is going to go. It becomes apparent that you are to be in the majority. You feel a general buzz of positive anticipation around you. Others notice it too.

The moon's days as a moon are numbered.

5c

"A LOT OF people miss the moon, Mr. Mollene. They blame you for taking away a beautiful part of the world."

"You know people have walked on the moon," said Mollene, "left garbage on the moon, crashed rockets into the moon. You know this?"

"But none of that made it any less beautiful."

"Sally didn't think so."

"Sally? Your wife?"

"My wife, yes. She loved the moon. Always had."

"I would think that after she died you would want to keep the moon in the sky to remind you of her. Why destroy something she loved so much?"

He puffed on his cigarette and stared at Alice for a few seconds. "It's not destroyed," he said.

"It might as well be. No one can see it. Why did you do that?"

"I have my reasons."

"What are they?"

"Next question, please."

Alice wanted the answer to the last question but knew that if she pushed, he was probably going to see her out the door and into the dark moonless night.

"There's been a lot of speculation about what the material is. Care to comment?"

He flicked ashes from his cigarette into a glass ashtray at his elbow. "I had a lot of scientists working on this project you know. People think I'm the only one who wanted the moon hidden, but it's not true. Bigwigs in the astronomical community begged to work on this project. They came up with the plan, I implemented it. The pepper's nothing but ash. Black, cold, ash."

"Do you ever look up at the moon and wish it was still there?"

"It is there."

"But it looks like it has disappeared."

"When I'm dead and gone, all you survivors who love the moon so much, you can go there and vacuum up the ash. It won't matter to me then."

6a

THE PLANE LANDS. I am escorted to a large meeting room. No chance to rest or clean myself up. By this time I am tired.

No matter. We have a date with destiny.

I arrive at a room filled with people. All kinds of people. My task force. Someone grabs me and whisks me to a table. They slap a name tag on me. Everyone chattering and yammering about the moon. Crazy moon.

Someone asks me why I'm there. I tell him I want to save the moon. He looks at me like I'm ill.

Someone else sees my name tag. "Hey," she says, "wasn't your grandfather on the moon missions?"

"Yeah," I say. "Ground crew."

"What would he think of all this?"

I rub my eyes. Am I really here? Does any of this matter at all? Shouldn't we be knocking those comets out of the sky and bringing the moon back? She's ours, after all. Born of the Earth. Made of the same stuff as the ground we walk on.

"I don't know," I say. "I wish someone would go to the moon and take care of this."

"But no one can. Not since the Chinese tried, and that was a while ago."

I knew that. Three missions they sent, all of them ended in

complete failure, the death of all three crews. After that no one wanted to do it anymore. No one had the appetite for more disaster on that scale.

But a long time ago people did do it. They ramped up Apollo in less than ten years. Couldn't we do it again?

I spent a long time on the task force. We debated endlessly, tying to come up with a recommendation for the country.

In the end, we decided to let it go. All of our proposed schemes to get it back would be too expensive. No nation could afford it, even with help from others. You know that. You look up in the sky now and don't see a moon.

It wasn't always like that. It didn't have to be like that. But the moon was not a priority. We let it go.

6b

WHEN THE COMMITTEE finally renders their decision, it is almost anti-climax. You cheer and holler along with everyone else. The moon is no longer the moon. She is our sister planet.

You are hailed as the man who erased the moon.

You try to wear the distinction with honor.

6c

"I SEE," SAID Alice. "May I make an observation?"

"Go ahead," Mollene said with his mouth a half smile.

"I think you are the most selfish and arrogant man that ever lived. You have a broken heart. Well boo hoo. You're not the first one. Are you so weak that you take away one of the most beautiful objects in existence just to ease your pain a little? I think you are terrible."

Mollene let his half smile broaden into a full smile, then a laugh. "If I was just a couple of decades younger," he said, "I'd ask you to marry me."

"I would never say yes."

"You do know how rich I am, don't you?"

Alice stood up and prepared to leave.

Mollene stopped her. "Wait," he said.

Something in his voice made her reconsider. She stopped.

"I'm sorry," he said. "That remark was uncalled for. Will you forgive me?"

She didn't say anything. Merely returned to her seat.

"I have wondered myself if what I did was right. I have done many good things in my life. I have sunk billions into renewable energy, and I have sunk more billions into fighting disease. Both were big important things. I am proud of them."

"I know all about those projects," said Alice. "Your name will go down in history as one of the world's greatest benefactors based on those two initiatives."

Mollene nodded. "Yes, I did all that for humanity. But this one thing. This moon erasure. It was for me."

"I am aware of that as well," said Alice. "Just because you can do a thing, does not mean you should."

Mollene leaned forward. "Did you ever look at the face of the moon?" he said.

Alice thought back. "In pictures," she said.

"The moon had a complexion. It looked like someone."

Alice noted Mollene's suddenly urgent tone. He was telling her something important. "That someone," said Alice. "Was it Sally?"

Mollene nodded. "I saw her features there. In the face of the moon. I had to blot them out. It was too painful to see her all the time, every month, staring down at me. As I said before, people can take the ash away after I'm gone. But until then, I don't want to look at the moon's face. I'm hoping you can understand that. Maybe you can help your readers to understand it as well."

7a

I FINISHED MY stint with the task force. Such a waste of time. There was no will for the moon. I wouldn't have believed it myself if I had not seen it firsthand.

I looked up at the night sky a few months later. The moon was still there, but it was smaller. A miniature version of its true self.

125

I tried saying goodbye to the moon, but I could not find the words.

7b

YOU FINISH YOUR time on the case. You get back to some kind of normal routine in your life. You step outside late one night, just to look up at the sky. You see the familiar silvery disk and realize you are not looking at the moon. Because of you and your efforts, you now gaze upon a planet. The Earth's sister planet, Luna. You feel a sense of profound loss, merely because of a designation. A *name*.

You wonder if it is possible to reverse the decision.

You wonder if you can bring the moon back.

7c

ALICE FINISHED HER interview with Richard Mollene. She returned to the gate and retrieved her bag from the guard, who touched the brim of his cap in greeting. She walked to her car. Just before she got into the driver's seat, she looked up at the sky again. The moon was now almost on the horizon. She could barely make out its face, almost as black as the night sky, but not *quite*.

"Good night, Sally," she whispered. "I hope you sleep well."

The Universe of Death

FIRST OFF, DESPITE my name, I didn't kill Amelia. Or Henry. So let's get that out of the way right now. You might be reading this and thinking I killed them. But look at the evidence if you can. It wasn't me.

Henry, when he was in his demented state, sometimes accused me of attempting to orchestrate Amelia's demise, but I had nothing to do with it. How could I? She died before I was created.

Also, I didn't ask to be brought on this expedition. This journey between the galaxies. That was all Henry's doing. He didn't want to be lonely on his voyage so he created me and gave me the attributes he thought I should have.

I am a *symbol*, after all, and as such, have always been part of the natural order of things, the cycle of becoming and ceasing to be, which, if you want to blame anything, you will have to start with the entity or process that started it all some unimaginably long time ago.

They call me Death. Or rather, you called me Death, and you clothed me in a dark robe with a hood so you couldn't see my face. My bony face, fleshless and white enough to scare you with the knowledge that my kin resided in you. The bones that hold you in place are the same bones holding me up. Death lives in you and you cannot bear the thought.

Henry liked to say that I have always been here, pre-dating

everything else, but Henry didn't always know what he was talking about. He thought he was immortal. Ho ho. No one is immortal. You can live a million, a billion years, and there is no guarantee you will live another day. Got that? Life is always conditional. There is no assurance that you will continue on for another nanosecond, let alone long enough to do what you want to do.

I have Henry to blame for bringing me here, and blame him. I do. There was no reason to invoke my form except to make himself feel as though he was some kind of clever man, bringing death to bear on his attempt to outlive the cosmos.

Even my existence is conditional. There's a big black button on the wall down the hall. Press it, and my app gets deleted. Henry's idea of a joke. Underneath it, another big button, red. Press that one and Amelia gets deleted. Henry liked seeing those buttons there. Gave him a sense of power.

He was riding on a starship between the galaxies and he needed me and Amelia for comfort. And he needed those buttons for comfort as well. Life and death together. Who can understand humans?

Before we go on, and before you begin to think me insane, I will acknowledge that I am a clever representation. A simulacrum conjured out of holographic apps stained with a generous helping of myth and tradition, not to mention Henry's particular brand of fear. He chose an ancient conception of death as a clattering old bone pile draped in dark cloth. I know this. Henry made me. Henry held me up as his creation. Or at least his recreation. He laughed when he talked to me. I made my voice as ominous as possible when I talked back. And he laughed some more. And laughed and laughed.

Good thing it didn't get on my nerves. Not that I have any. Ha ha.

Henry tried to give me humor. I'm not sure he succeeded at all.

I THINK IT was maybe a million or so years ago that people first started getting an inkling that the universe was going to run down into a flat line of dissipated energy as the big bang entropied to its dismal conclusion. This troubled some at the time, but not too many. After all, that was going to be a long time in the future. Maybe longer than anything conscious could possibly exist. But time passed and people acquired more life for themselves. They got really good at life extension and began to pile up birthdays in the four, five, and six figures.

And then things changed. They started to see the day when all that remained of the universe would be nothing but themselves and they found this to be supremely troubling.

So they devised a scheme. A grand project that would save the universe.

Here was the problem in a nutshell: The universe had only one complete set of atoms, and it was apparently an insufficient set to contract the whole enterprise.

But these people, these human beings, were not willing to accept that there was no answer to getting more of the universe. They reasoned thus: The universe is really a distribution scheme. There is all this matter with each atom distributed along time lines, a branch for each particle. Very neat and tidy. Very arranged. But it meant that matter was too sparsely spread out and the big bang would peter out.

Enter human ingenuity.

Here was their solution: Collect up some of those atoms from the past and bring them forward in time. Just go back in time a few nanoseconds down a branch and pluck the atom there and shoot it forward. Go down another nanosecond, pluck the atom and shoot it forward. Repeat indefinitely. Before long, you will have billions, trillions, of copies of that atom all residing in the here and now. Do it a sufficient number of times with a sufficient number of atoms in their timelines and you will add enough mass to tip the balance of the universe in favor of slowing down the big bang.

You will contract time and space, eventually making the universe fall back into a big crunch where the whole shooting match can start up again.

Reincarnation on the grandest scale possible.

Oh, it was a grand scheme. The grandest of all.

They deployed the tiny time machines all over the galaxy, and even beyond the galaxy. Each one began pumping atoms from the past into the future. The mass of the universe increased steadily.

And when it became clear, over the next few centuries, that the project was going to work, people began to think about where they wanted to be when the big crunch came. It was no trivial issue. The brightest minds of the day saw that some locations were going to be annihilated into nothing, but other locations were going to afford people passage into the new universe on the other side of the big crunch with much of their structure undamaged. Or, at least, undamaged enough to be reconstructed in the new universe.

And human existence became a game of jockeying for position. People built their own starships and boarded them and rode out to these remote outposts where they could survive the big crunch.

No one wanted to be left out of the big crunch. Everyone wanted their patterns to survive into the next cycle.

See, no one wants to die if they don't have to. Not even me.

I'M REMEMBERING A time long ago. Me and Henry together on the starship. We spent time together in those days, talking about things. What else did we have to do?

"You know," said Henry, "I hesitated before bringing you here."

"Indeed," I said. We were sitting on comfy chairs in the observation bubble. The Milky Way galaxy spiraled behind us, filling a third of the sky. "Who would want death as a traveling companion?"

"It wasn't just that," said Henry. "I wasn't sure you could really help me."

I turned to him, my bones scraping against one another, my robe rustling. "Well, Henry, old pal. I think your instincts were right. I can't."

Henry laughed. "No, that's where you're wrong. People are funny creatures. We need reminders to keep us going. I needed to be reminded of death. That's why you are here. You make me think of what will become of me if I don't succeed at what I am trying to do."

I tilted my head at him. "Thank you for damning me to an eternity of boredom so that you can be fulfilled."

"I really should have gotten rid of that sarcastic streak some time ago," said Henry. "It does get tiresome."

Tiresome? *I* was tiresome? It seemed to me that *everything* was tiresome. I rose from my chair, picked up my scythe and walked with it to the bubble of glass separating me from space only an inch or so from my face. No steam clouded the view. I, of course, did not experience respiration.

Black space extended as far as possible. We had been traveling for much longer than I could possibly imagine. Henry lived a hermit's life and liked it.

And yet, he sometimes needed companionship. He occasionally brought back Amelia and spent a few days with her. Until the pain of her loss overcame the pleasure he felt in being with a copy of her. Not to mention the shame of resurrecting a dead girlfriend and what that did to his psyche.

So he would let her go and be alone again, except for me. He would always come back and sit with me in the observation lounge. He liked the blackness, I think. He had a strange fascination for the emptiness of it all.

"I should think that everything would be tiresome to you now," I said. "Why exert the energy to go on, Henry? Why bother?"

I had asked him this question many times. I believe he had fixed it so I would ask this question. It was part of his strange need. Usually he did not try to answer. Sometimes he would offer some convoluted and unconvincing reply, referring to the need for life to continue, that the whole purpose of the universe had always been to promote and sustain life. This never moved me. So I waited. And this time there was no reply. Henry rose from his own chair and walked away from the observation deck and down the hall. I knew what he was up to.

Lately he had been feeling even more melancholy over the loss of Amelia. She was, after all, the woman from his past who made him feel as though life had meaning. That was the way he had always put it to me. But Amelia had died several thousand years ago in a ghastly accident involving an explosion as she was tending one of the early tiny time machines, the ones that humans had been deploying around the galaxy. Something went wrong with the calibration settings and instead of a steady trickle of atoms from the past, a flood of them came streaming out, exploding her area of space with a small big bang of its own. Poor Amelia's atoms were scattered across space. Very tragic.

I had nothing to do with it, I hasten to emphasize. I am a myth, after all, created by people to try to understand and perhaps assuage their sense of loss and betrayal when such accidents occur.

Do you believe this, you who are reading this, presumably after the big crunch has crunched and the successor big bang has banged? Do you have any idea of what we are doing here and now?

FOR ODD SYMBOLISM you probably can't beat me watering Henry's garden. He liked me to use an old fashioned watering can and his wish was my urge so there it was: me holding a classic tin watering can showering his soybeans, carrots, beets, and peas with moisture. Was this the most effective means of keeping his food requirements intact? Probably not. But what a picture. My bony fingers clinking against the tin handle. My robe dragging along the leaves. Me bending over as if to smell the earth there.

We sped along at better than several million miles per hour toward our destination between galaxies. Henry wanted his pattern to survive the universe. Such a strange wish, really. Who was Henry to survive? Who was any person to survive? Henry once said bodies don't matter. It's all about pattern. He said I was just as real as he was, because I was made of pattern.

Oh, such nonsense from the mouth of Henry.

I don't want you to get the wrong idea about Henry. He was fine with having a body. His time spent with Amelia attests to that.

They didn't spend their days discussing the theory and practice of expanding universes, I can tell you that. And while they were occupied with their activities, I went about maintaining the ship and its environs.

The ship is, as I'm sure you will have guessed, mostly self-sustaining. But there are adjustments to be made here and there to maintain the balance of energy and food and air and such. Henry graciously taught me all the ins and outs of shipboard duties. I performed my tasks admirably.

As I was finishing up my daily chores one evening I heard a sound and a rustle behind me. "Another good time with Amelia?" I asked in my best snotty voice.

"Henry is indisposed." A female voice.

I turned. Amelia walked toward me. An electric hiccup went through me, as though the universe had shuddered.

"What are you doing here?" I asked.

"I've been begging Henry to let me go for some time," she said. "He kept refusing so I arranged things to make them work out better for me."

"I see," I said.

"Henry will not be with us on this journey any longer."

I tried to see my way clear to the end of my days. "What are you saying?" I asked. I found myself trembling, ever so slightly. My robes rustled and my bones chattered. I never knew those machinations were predicated by fear, but I experienced an opening up of meaning in the world at that precise instant.

"Here's the problem," said Amelia. "How does one kill Death?"

She wanted to terminate me? She wanted *me* gone? "You aren't even real," I said. "You're just a copy that Henry made, a copy of someone who died centuries ago."

I was fully aware that I was in the same situation. But, you see, I was different. I was Henry's friend. Indeed, you might say that I *was* Henry in a certain way of being, since he designed me to amuse him and only him.

"You can believe I'm a copy if you wish," said Amelia. "But then, what does that say about you?"

She had me there. We were both unreal simulacrums, were we not? Perhaps it would have been best to ally ourselves with each other. Two strange beings adrift in the cosmos, hurtling toward a rendezvous with the next universe. Perhaps our patterns would survive through the crunch and be reincarnated on the other side, after the big bang.

But that didn't happen.

Instead, I experienced this awful feeling for the first time in my existence. I wanted Amelia dead. She had dispatched the only other entity in my universe and I hated her for it.

Oh, I know what you are thinking. That was Henry's doing. He tweaked the app so I would feel that way.

And what of it? Just because a feeling is manufactured does not make it any the less potent. We both knew where the controls for our apps were.

We bolted for the wall down the hall.

WELL, I SUPPOSE I won't keep you in suspense any longer. Amelia reached the app delete buttons first and kept me away so I couldn't reach hers. She hovered her hand over mine, threatening to press it if I advanced any closer. She was stronger than me and faster. More muscles. Much better fleshed out, if you will. I was powerless to defeat her.

So I didn't kill her. Exactly as I had said at the beginning.

She's allowing me this final testament before she terminates me. Says I've been in existence for so many centuries that I deserved some kind of memorial.

Did Henry put that into her app, or did she arrange her own simulacrum of compassion? No way to tell, now. She had a hand in collapsing the universe, and paid the ultimate price. I suppose it's only fitting that she survive and I get to take my chances with the passage from big crunch to big bang.

Poor Henry. Amelia told me she killed him, but it wasn't an act of passion on her part. Henry wanted to die. He was sick of living so long. Who could blame him? He had Amelia choke him to death. I can only imagine the pain that the simulacrum of Amelia feels about that.

Just a few minutes ago I performed my last task for him. I made a simulacrum of him.

He and Amelia appear to be very happy.

Or should I say, the copy of Henry appears to be very happy with the copy of Amelia?

I think they plan to delete the app that is me with a simultaneous pressing of the delete button.

Listen for me. Listen for all of us. We'll be riding the wave of the big bang, the next one, I hope. We all hope.

I'll end my account here, while I can still listen to my robes rustle and my bones rattle.

Such pleasant sounds.

The Clex Are Our Friends

INTRODUCTION

YOU ARE ON the winning side of a prolonged and bloody interplanetary conflict.

Congratulations!

You can thank your planet and its glorious principles, your commanding officers, your buddies in arms, and yourself.

Now for the next phase.

You have been ordered into Cleck, the battlefield planet, to help restore order and civil society. You will encounter alien races and alien customs.

Many of these will be confusing. What's worse, many of them will be dangerous. This booklet will attempt to help you with both situations, as well as prepare you for your mission.

This booklet is encrypted so only you can read it. Do not fear a security breach if it should fall into alien hands. However, do exercise prudent caution and discretion in its use.

It is to your advantage to study the contents of this booklet very carefully. Your life may depend on it.

Also, remember at all times that you are a representative of Earth. Please uphold the highest standards of morality and conduct.

SOME HISTORY

YOU ARE ON Cleck to do a vital job; namely: secure the planet.

Of course, this simple statement does not convey the full flavor of your duties.

Allow me, in this short space and in my own way, to explain more fully the parameters of your mission.

Your duty on Cleck is to remove any Stewn left behind after the final battle of the war.

As you may or may not know, Stewn are descended from Clex. Centuries ago the Clex developed space travel. Some of the Clex left their planet to colonize another. Those migrant Clex evolved into Stewn.

A few years ago, the Stewn returned to the planet Cleck to claim what they thought was rightfully theirs. This included massive mineral deposits, which the Clex have since graciously offered to us in exchange for cleaning up the Stewn. This is indeed a fortunate circumstance for which we as a planet can be grateful. All we have to do is come in and mine it out. After the Stewn are gone.

It goes without saying that the Stewn invasion of Cleck was completely contrary to accepted norms of interstellar law. Earth stepped in to stop the invasion and right a terrible wrong. Our motive was the restoration of justice.

We lost a lot of good people in the process. Some may have been your comrades.

But it was worth it. The Clex needed us. They really did.

So here we are. Revel in your duties. Accept the accolades that are sure to be showered upon you.

EQUIPMENT

TRANSLATOR. YOU HAVE been issued a translation device. Keep it on your person at all times. The Clex are a touchy species. If they believe you do not understand them, they are liable to grab you with some vehemence and may inadvertently tear off one of your limbs. This will upset them terribly. Also, make sure your translation device has fresh batteries.

GOGGLES. Air on Cleck is very moist and has a high acidic content. This does not bother the Clex, but will make your eyes burn if you are exposed to it too long. The specially designed goggles you have been issued will alleviate this problem.

MRE. You can't eat Clex food. If you tried, it would eat you. Bring your own food.

The above items are in addition to your standard gear, NOT a replacement for same.

FIRST CONTACT

CLEX HAVE VERY long tongues. Two of them each. Upon first meeting you, they will extend one or more of their tongues, place them on your person, and taste you for several seconds. Do not be alarmed. Few of your fellow soldiers have succumbed to the corrosive juices that coat a Clex tongue. And the ones that did weren't wearing proper gear no matter what rumors you've heard.

After the tasting, be sure to spit on the ground. This is their custom, and by doing so you convey the message that you respect their customs.

Your spitting will elicit strange buzzing noises from the Clex. Our intelligence has convinced us that this is their equivalent of laughter. It is an indication that they appreciate the expulsion of saliva. Use this fact to help you. Those soldiers who do not spit sometimes end up in sick bay with severe injuries.

CLEX CHARACTER

WE KNOW YOU'VE heard stories about the Clex. That they are cowardly, that they eat children, and that they will not defend themselves. Don't you believe it. It has been widely reported that no Clex has ever been seen eating its own child. Not once.

Also, while it is true that they cowered in their cities while their enemies, the Stewn, rained destruction across their planet, when it came time, the Clex were very willing to help us defeat the Stewn. They offered us unlimited access to their food stores, even though we could not eat any of them, and they tended to some of our wounded when we could not get to them. A few of those even survived.

You may also hear rumors that the Clex resent our presence. Nothing could be further from the truth. They respect our fighting ability and our amazing spirit and skills.

The cold hard truth is this: Clex can fight but usually choose not to because of their religious beliefs, which include a strong pacifist streak.

Recall our devotion to religious freedom. It is a cornerstone of a humanitarian society. Do not mock or criticize the Clex for adhering to their religious principles, even if it puts you in danger. You're a soldier. You live for danger, right?

Remember, we are here to help the Clex, not to judge them.

FAMILY LIFE

AFTER INITIAL CONTACT with a Clex, you may be invited into their homes. Accept the invitation gracefully.

The Clex couple constantly. Several times a day. Your presence in their house will not deter them. Try not to comment. Also, try not to watch. For your own good.

Once in a Clex home, you will be pounced on by their children. Do not be alarmed. Few of them are lethal. Slimy and smelly, but not lethal.

Clex generally have many children. Each house will harbor at least a dozen, often more. This does not mean they breed uncontrollably. On the contrary, they could in fact have dozens more children than they do, but they restrain themselves to help preserve the resources of their planet. Such an attitude is well worthy of our respect.

You will sometimes be offered one or more of their children as a gift. If this happens, you must immediately hit the button on your translator marked with the big NO in bright red glowing letters. The phrase that comes out of it will be the Clex version of the following:

"I greatly appreciate your kind offer but must decline at this time. I hope you understand."

Practice hitting this button rapidly and accurately.

The Clex like to sing. At first their songs will be hard on your ears. Think of pigs going to slaughter. Mixed with fingernails on chalkboard. Sound disgusting? Well, music is an acquired taste. You'll get used to it.

FIELD WORK

ALTHOUGH IT IS fun and instructive, not to mention horizon broadening, to spend time with aliens and alien culture, do not forget your reason for being on Cleck. Be as polite as necessary to the Clex, but keep your wits about you and focus on the mission.

Which is killing Stewn.

The best way to kill a Stewn is by blunt force. You have been issued a metal baton for this purpose. If you should lose it, a heavy stick will do. You can find an abundant assortment of good strong sticks in the Cleck countryside. They will have thorns on them. Wear your gloves.

Stewn used to congregate in great flocks, gathering in more or less exposed locations to launch their attacks on Clex houses and towns. That was before we defeated them. Now they generally cower in caves and such.

This one fact solves the issue of telling a Clex from a Stewn. Clex are our friends and greet us openly. Stewn hide. Burn this fact into your brain, because, honestly, there's no other way to tell them apart. They look almost identical.

I don't need to tell you that looks can be deceiving. Clex are our friends. Stewn are our enemies. Very simple.

By the time you see them, the Stewn will be mostly unarmed. Many will be feeble from lack of food. After all, we cut off their supply lines.

A good number of the Stewn will be close to death when you find them anyway, so you may think of your actions as being merciful. Humanitarian would be a good word to keep in mind. Especially when you return to Earth after your mission and are asked about your activities by civilians.

Remember not to disturb the Clex while you go about your

duties. They do not like to be bothered with such things. The Clex, as you may have surmised from what you have read so far, are a very refined and honorable species. They are expected to be a great help to us when we gather our forces to invade the Stewn home planet.

With luck, you will be part of that campaign, but do not get ahead of yourself. That is at least a year or so in the future.

SOME CAUTIONS

OCCASIONALLY A CLEX will offer to accompany you on your missions. This is a tricky situation. In general it is best to discourage such participation; however, certain individual Clex can be persistent and persuasive.

Here is the problem: Once a Stewn gets within smelling distance of a Clex, all its latent hostility and murderous intent rises to the surface and you have a very dangerous Stewn on your hands.

The remedy is to keep Clex away from Stewn. If a Clex offers to help, use your NO button. If that does not work, allow the Clex to come with you, but dispatch it at your earliest opportunity.

Away from any prying eyes.

You will thank yourself later.

SOME FINAL THOUGHTS

RUMORS ARE A part of military life. We understand this. We know you hear many distasteful stories about Clex society and Clex as a species.

Try to ignore these. They will only poison your attitude and make you reluctant to carry out your very important duties.

Remember that the Clex are our friends. As such, we do not betray or hurt them unless absolutely necessary for the good of the mission, which, ultimately, is for their good as well.

Use your superior intellect and killing power with discretion. Harm a Clex only when circumstances make all other options unfeasible.

THANK YOU

FINALLY, ON BEHALF of a grateful planet, which will benefit tremendously from your brave and necessary mission, let me offer my heartfelt thanks for your unselfish and unflinching duty.

You make us all proud to be human.

They Taste Like Chicken

FIRST TIME I saw them was with my best friend Dan. It was hunting season and we were driving up north in the Giff. That's the Gifford Pinchot National Forest, for those unfamiliar with Southwestern Washington State. We were looking to bag us a deer, maybe an elk, and we were tooling up Wind River Highway just before dawn with Mount Saint Helens in front of us like a princess in white. Dan's headlights caught a couple of shapes and then two fawn-sized critters shot out from the woods right in front of us. Dan hollered: "What the fu—" but didn't finish the phrase before we hit both of them—smack! splat!—with the front of Dan's truck. We looked at each other.

"What were those things?" I said.

"Beats me," said Dan.

He stopped the truck a quarter mile past impact and put it into reverse. I listened to the engine strain and whine, like it didn't want to go backwards that far.

Two lumps on the side of the road were waiting for us. I got out of the truck before Dan stopped it completely. It was still cold and wet outside. Typical November in the Giff. I walked over to the road kill and bent down to take a look.

These two things, whatever they were, were nothing like anything I'd ever seen. For one thing, their blood wasn't red. It had come out of their eyes and some of it dripped from the other end and it was this kind of golden color. Odd, to say the least. And their eyes, they were big, like owl eyes. Like they had been living somewhere so dark that they needed gigantic eyes just to get around. Their heads were kind of bear-like, but the snout was more elongated than a bear. Their paws were kind of cat-like, but again, longer than a cat's would be. And their bodies were like roundish balls.

I heard Dan come stand beside me. "That's some smell they got," he said.

Dan was right. They exuded a sweet aroma. Like sugary donuts wafting honeyed air in our direction. Got my mouth watering like I was smelling bacon frying in the morning.

"Any idea what these things are?" I said.

Dan picked one up by the tail, which also was not like any tail I had ever seen on any animal. It was pointy, like a whittled stick, and it had no fur on it, unlike the rest of the thing, which was covered in this silky kind of golden fur, smooth as anything. Made me think of the softest leather when I touched it.

Dan grabbed up the other one and tossed them both into the back of his truck. They made a nice thunking sound. It was weird. Everything about these critters made me feel good. I don't know if that makes sense, but there it is.

"Let's go home," said Dan. "I want to find out what these things taste like."

Dan and me, we don't cut short a hunting trip for nothing. But I didn't put up any objection.

"Sounds good to me," I said.

DAN LIVED IN the woods. A real mountain man, or as close to one as you could get in this day and age. His cabin was wood heated. No electricity. His bathroom was an outhouse behind the cabin, and he liked to talk about the coming collapse of, well, everything. I lived a few miles away on the Columbia River in Cedar Falls. We were from different worlds, but hunting season put us on the same map every year.

We pulled into Dan's driveway. "I'll get the stove going," he said. "You get these critters skinned and ready for the skillet."

"I'm on it," I said. I went around back of the truck and lifted our trophies by their tails and carried them to the shed behind Dan's cabin and slammed them down on the work table. I took a knife from the wall and started skinning one of them.

I started noticing weird things right away. For example, I expected the skin to be soft, like a rabbit's, but instead it was tougher than anything I had ever cut into. Made a bear's hide seem like butter. I really had to grip the knife hard and saw at the hide. Once I got going, it peeled back pretty easy, but then I got more surprised. The muscles were gold. Crazy. What had gold-colored muscles? And the guts were all mixed up. I think I saw only one lung, if that's what it was. Two hearts. Small ones, so I guess that's why there were two. Then toward the intestines, I found a few globules of organs that I couldn't guess what they were. I scooped all of that stuff out and dropped the mess into a bucket next to Dan's work table.

Dan came in. "You ready with that meat?" he said. His eyes were ablaze. I'd never seen him that way.

"Still working on it," I said.

"I'll get going on the other one," he said, and took another knife and started gutting his animal. We worked feverishly, skinning and dressing the things. It was as if we couldn't do anything else. We had to taste these things. *Had* to. Like our lives depended on it.

The muscles came off the bones pretty easy. We got some little steaks from the hindquarters, and long strips of bacon-like stuff from the bellies and pretty nice lengths of muscles from the legs.

"I've never been so hungry in my life," said Dan.

"Me neither," I said. "What *are* these things?"

"No idea," said Dan.

We took the meat into the kitchen, where Dan had gotten a big pot of water going, with onions, celery, and carrots, and we threw in chunks of the meat, which immediately turned a bright orange, almost fluorescent, then gradually migrated to a more gentle bright red.

The rest we put into a big greased pan, frying up pieces of our critters and sending this *smell* into the air. It was like the arms of the flavor gods all reached down from the clouds and punched our taste buds until they cried for the love of the world. Sounds batty, doesn't it? But I felt it. That divine spark of flavor. These creatures, these cuts of meat, did not come from this planet. Couldn't have.

"How done should it get?" said Dan.

"No idea," I said. "Probably safest to cook it right through. Don't know what kind of parasites they might have."

"I see your point," said Dan, "but I don't think I can wait. These things are going to taste out of this world."

Dan is a man of precise words. "Out of this world" was not a metaphor for him. It meant something.

While the meat sizzled and, as it were, snaked its aroma around the room and into our nostrils and kind of did a number on our brains, I asked Dan what he meant by that.

"You remember those lights in the sky a few days ago?" he said.

I remembered. Some people in the Giff reported UFOs and strange doings north of Wind Mountain and into the Falling Creek area, which was not five miles from Dan's cabin. "You see any of that?" I asked Dan.

Dan nodded. "Damnedest thing, those lights. Never seen anything like them, and I've been living here twenty years."

"You don't believe in UFOs," I said to my friend Dan, whose head was torqued onto his shoulders about as tightly as anyone I had ever known.

"Doesn't matter what I believe or don't believe," he said. "Look at the facts. Those critters aren't from this world. Their biology is… different."

Well. I hear crazy things all the time. We got people in town who walk around talking to themselves and to people you can't see, but none of them are *Dan*. None of them got the smarts that

Dan— Oh, never mind. You get the idea, right? Dan was telling me these things we were about to eat were aliens. From another planet.

"This is crazy," I said.

"I know," he said.

"We could be, I don't know, violating some intergalactic law."

"Then they can come lock me up. *After* I taste what we killed."

"Accidentally killed," I said.

Dan waved his hand at me and went and got us a couple of plates. He pulled some slices of bread out of the oven that had turned to toast and put them on the plates. Then he scooped some of the fried meat onto the toast and handed me one of the plates. We couldn't even wait to get to the table. We stood there like the lame ass bachelors we were and ate standing up with those golden-red juices dripping down our fingers and onto our shirts. We didn't care.

First off, the texture. It felt just right in my mouth, like it wanted to live there. Tender, but not mushy, and it yielded to my teeth like it was meant to be chomped by me.

It tasted like chicken. I need to get that out of the way, first, because that was the familiar part. But then. Oh, my. It was not so much the taste that followed, it was more like a symphony of something playing with our heads. I caught hints of venison, salmon, bear, and other animals, but there was more than that. I also got this hit of coriander, some curry mixed in as well, but also this subtle stroke of cinnamon, like it wanted to seduce my tongue.

Dan noticed that too and we each took half a step away from one another. Then the flavors started getting even more unreal. They blended into this concoction of concentrated tastiness. I got zinged by sauerkraut, punched by heat, and looped around by its sweetness. The whole experience was almost too much for my taste buds, if you can believe that. The flavors seemed to go straight to my brain, where it bounced around and set off shooting stars of pleasure.

I had not tasted anything like these things. Ever.

Dan cleaned his plate and looked at me. "What the hell *was* that," he said.

I didn't have an answer for Dan. How could I? We finished up the fried meat and then, with scarcely any pause, we ladled out the stew and dug right in. If there was ever a chance that food could be addictive, we had found the crack that would do it for us. I guess, in a way, we were lucky we only had two of the things. If there were a hundred more, I think we would have tried to eat them all.

When the pot was empty and our plates and bowls were licked clean, we put down our spoons and forks and looked at each other.

"What just happened?" said Dan.

"We had first contact with aliens," I said. "And we ate them."

Dan nodded. "Think there's more of them out there in the Giff?"

I turned my head north, as if I could look through Dan's cabin to the woods on the other side. There was a lot of forest out there. Some people said Bigfoot lived there, even though almost no one, except loopy folks, ever actually claimed to see one. But, just for the sake of argument, if Bigfoot could live there, then surely a bunch of littlefeet like what we just ate could be hidden there too. Stands to reason.

We got in the truck and drove out to where we killed those first two. Dan parked way off the road and we grabbed our rifles and trudged into the woods. By this time the sun was up and it had mostly dried the wet off everything. We found the tracks of the littlefeet and they took us deeper into the forest. Ferns slapped at our thighs, and we pushed maple saplings aside. We were on the hunt, no doubt. The tracks indicated that the aliens waddled a little as they walked. Made sense. They were pretty chubby things. Thick with that sweet meat.

Dan and I didn't talk much as we walked. I asked him if he thought maybe we should let this alone. That maybe we shouldn't be trying to eat more aliens. He said, with perfect sense, that we had already crossed that line, so another few wouldn't make any difference. It sounded like the logic of a murderer, but I didn't argue with him. I had crossed that line too.

After a couple of miles we came to a clearing and that's where we found the ship.

Now, I don't expect you to believe me. I'm telling this story as much for myself as for whoever you are reading it, but if you've stuck with me this far, then you can go to the end with me.

The ship was small, much smaller than I thought it would be, given all the fuss that its lights made when it came into its landing. *Crash* landing, I might add. The thing was broken in two, like a medicine capsule might be split in two. It was maybe twenty feet long and three feet wide.

"This ain't the mother ship," said Dan.

I had to agree with him. We approached it with our rifles at the ready, but I think we already knew it was empty. It had this dead feeling about it, as if it had given up whatever life it once possessed.

When I got right up to it, I poked the thing with the barrel of my rifle. I expected to hear metal click against metal. Instead, the barrel sunk into the hull a few inches.

"Hey," I said. "The ship's soft. Like it's made of foam or something."

Dan nodded. "It's disintegrating," he said. "Won't be any sign of it soon."

"Well crap," I said. "That means we won't be able to preserve it."

"Looks like it," said Dan. He picked up a stick from the ground and stuck it into the interior of the vessel and pulled back, zipping the thing open like it was a plastic bag. The interior was already runny and beginning to smell. We saw hints of what might have been some structure: partitions, mostly, but also a place where protrusions from the wall seemed to give the impression of some kind of instrumentation.

"What do you make of that?" I asked Dan.

"What I make of it, is that there's room in this thing for at least a dozen of them critters."

I saw what Dan was getting at. We both knew we would eat those critters if we found them.

"I think we have to tell someone about this," I said.

"Tell who?" said Dan.

"Hell, I don't know. The *authorities*. Fish and Game. NASA. *Someone*. This—" I kicked at the ship "—vessel survived entry into our atmosphere enough that at least some of its passengers survived. And now it's melting away. The government should know about a material that does *that*."

Dan shook his head vigorously. "No no no," he said. "We don't want no federal agencies sticking their noses here. Would ruin life in these woods. *Ruin* it. You got me?"

Dan's eyes were lit *up*. I got him. I knew what he was about. He liked his mountain man life and didn't want anything disrupting it. He had plans, for when the collapse finally really and truly came, for blowing up the bridge on the Columbia, just to keep the riffraff from Portland out of his woods. He didn't like people around, is what I'm saying. I got that. But me? I was okay with people. Hell, I *liked* people. The more the better. My time with Dan, hunting in the fall, was more of a vacation than a way of life. But Dan is persuasive. His laconic ways. His directness. It's hard for me to contradict him.

"Okay," I said. "We keep this to ourselves. Looks like this ship's going to melt into the forest soon anyway. But…"

Dan looked at me. "But?" he said.

"We have to find the other passengers. The longer they're on the loose, the longer they're out of our stomachs."

Dan grinned about as wide as the milky way. "Now you're talking," he said.

I'M NOT PROUD of the decision we made, but as an excuse I offer the fact that we were intoxicated by the meat. Maybe not an excuse, exactly, but a reason. We spent the rest of that day and half the next in the woods around the crashed vessel. In between, we slept in the cab of Dan's truck, but only long enough to grab a few winks. Then we were back in the woods. We found tracks of littlefeet, followed them for a while, then lost them. We couldn't find a pattern to their wanderings and concluded they must have been lost or frightened. Probably both.

"You think they ended up here by accident?" I asked Dan.

Dan offered a philosophical pause before answering. "Could be they were jettisoned by the mother ship," he said. "Maybe they were pets and the owners got tired of them. Rather than put them down, they dropped them here as they passed by."

Oh, I know, it's crazy talk. As I'm putting down his words, I'm thinking we both must be loons. But back then, as it was happening, it all made perfect sense. Dan spent a lot of time thinking about things like that. He's got no television, for one thing, which frees up a lot of time for creative thought. So I thought it had some validity. Maybe a lot of validity.

But even for a couple of hunting veterans like us, a day and a half without bagging anything got old, and I stopped being curious about the littlefeet or their silly spaceship. We stopped trudging around in the woods and went back to the site of the crash. The ship had slipped even further into decay. It looked like a giant mushroom that was rotting in the rain. Bugs had arrived. Not to mention worms. Flies and disgusting crawling things were all over it.

"See," said Dan. "What did I tell you? It'll be gone in no time."

I saw his point, but I was seized by a sadness I couldn't explain. It seemed so wrong for the thing to disappear without a trace. I stood there for a long time, contemplating the injustice of life and death until Dan slapped me on the chest.

"What?" I said.

"Let's get home," he said. "I'm hungry."

"Yeah," I said. "Let's go." But there was no vim or vigor behind my words. I knew all Dan had were a few packages of last year's deer jerky and some bread and vegetables. He had no littlefeet meat, and that seemed even sadder than the melting spaceship.

We rode back in silence. The bumps in the road jostled us in our seats and made the cab seem like a coffin, the way it enclosed us. Kept us in. Oh, I know I'm sounding a little loopy right here, but I'm just telling you what it was like. It felt like we were going to a funeral.

We got back to Dan's cabin about mid afternoon. I was figuring out a way to let him know that I didn't much want to hang around and I was going to go home and heat up some canned soup and feel sorry for myself, when Dan brought the truck to a stop and we just sat in the cab and looked out the windshield and what should we see but about half a dozen littlefeet milling around in front of the truck.

Dan's eyes lit up. "Holy shit," he whispered. He reached behind the seat where our rifles were stowed and brought his weapon around and carefully opened his door and put one foot out onto the ground. I also grabbed my rifle, but then I did something that changed everything.

I looked at the littlefeet.

They had dragged some of the entrails of the ones we had skinned the day before. From what I could see, it looked like they were trying to bury the guts of their friends. A few of them had begun to dig into the ground, but they were having difficulty because their feet were not claw-like at all. Their planet probably didn't have ground like we did. Or maybe their planet had different ground. Oh, hell. I don't know what I'm talking about. All I know is that they were trying to do something with the guts of their friends. Something ritualistic.

"Hey Dan," I said. "Hold up."

I didn't have to say anything to Dan, though. He saw it too. Probably saw it before I did. He put down his rifle and just sat there, staring at the aliens.

"I'll be damned," he said.

Well, to make a long story short, Dan and I got a pair of shovels and we dug a hole out back on his property. The littlefeet milled around us the whole time, like we were their friends. They must have known we killed and ate their buddies. I mean, they *must* have. But maybe they understood in some alien way we couldn't understand. Like they knew it was an accident, kind of?

We covered up the hole and patted the earth down. That aroma was there. Filled the air. Made my mouth water again, but what could I do? I didn't have the heart to brain the things after that. They came to Dan's cabin because they knew one of theirs was dead and they had to take care of that.

"It's a universal thing," said Dan in his most philosophical voice. "Love and death, my friend. Life is always about love and death."

We had a moment of silence. The littlefeet understood immediately and joined in. Then Dan turned to the group of littlefeet, huddled together against the chill air, and asked them if there was anywhere he could take them.

Like they could answer. But it didn't matter. They seemed to understand. They climbed into the back of Dan's truck. I went into Dan's cabin and returned with the last of his deer jerky and opened the jar and passed it around the group. The littlefeet took to it right away. They dug right in, chomping and salivating like Dan and I did the day before. I felt a little guilty about eating their friends. Dan could tell. He told me I needed to get over that.

He was right.

I half expected Dan to change his mind and shoot them all so we could have a feast, but that didn't happen. Dan has his faults, but murder isn't one of them.

We drove out past Mount Saint Helens to a remote spot Dan and I knew about. An old abandoned logging road took us even further into the woods and Dan stopped the truck and we got out and he opened the gate of his truck.

The littlefeet scrambled out and jumped to the ground. They ran around our feet for a few seconds, then retreated and stood staring at us with those giant eyes.

"They should be able to hunt okay in the dark," I said.

"You're right about that," said Dan.

"They've got a taste for deer now."

Dan nodded. "They should be able to pull one down if they work together."

"I'm still not sure we're doing the right thing. These could be the ultimate invasive species," I said.

"They'll be fine here," said Dan.

Before the littlefeet turned around and left us, one of them approached us with something in its teeth. At first I couldn't tell what it was, but as it got closer, I saw it was actually two identical items. They were small sculptures of two littlefeet, studded with turquoise and rose stones. The material was gold, as far as I could tell, though my knowledge of metal is not expansive. Maybe a gold alloy. The littlefoot dropped them to the ground, then turned and the bunch of them waddled off together into the forest. Dan and I watched them for a time, then I bent down and picked up the sculptures.

"Nice work," said Dan. "If people ever get to the point where they would accept them—"

"And not want to eat them," I said.

"—and not want to eat them," said Dan. He cleared his throat. As much to clear the thought of their flavor as to gather his thoughts. "They could have a future in the jewelry business."

I agreed with my friend Dan. I've worn that sculpture on a chain around my neck ever since. Dan hung his from a string on the rear view mirror of his truck.

We've never seen the littlefeet again, but we know they're out in the woods somewhere. We hope.

And I've only regretted not eating them a few times.

Well, maybe half a dozen.

The Last Last Meal

ME AND MY wife Liz have a restaurant on the edge of our little town. Nothing fancy. Lots of fried stuff. Also sandwiches, burgers, gravy. Our vegetable is coleslaw drenched in mayo. Our desserts come loaded with sugar and chocolate. All designed to put you into a carbo coma, the best kind of daze there is. We are your basic greasy spoon, and proud of it.

We have a reputation. Even among the inmates at the penitentiary a few miles out of town. The guards have lunch at our place, and some have dinner after their shifts. We lard them up pretty good and they seem to like it. I guess they talk to the inmates about us, because when it comes time for the last meals of the condemned, more often that not they want something from our place.

Their tastes, in their final hours, usually run to fried chicken, lots of it. Also French fries (again: generous with the portions). And don't forget slabs of cake and quarts of ice cream served with dripping chocolate sauce. You want to know what people really want to eat? Just ask someone who's never going to eat again.

Along about the beginning of fall one night, with the wind getting chilly and the leaves starting to crackle some, one of the rolly polly guards sauntered into our place about 6:30 and handed Liz a handwritten list. He'd been in the place before, getting last meal orders.

"This for you?" I heard Liz ask. She was waiting on tables. I was in the back, keeping up with orders.

"Nope," said the guard. "For Michael Rand. One of the walking dead."

I heard Liz whistle. "This is some order," she said.

"Yup," said the guard. "Too late for him to worry about his cholesterol, I guess."

He didn't laugh, but Liz did. "Even so," she said. "Six orders of fish and chips? And a whole chocolate cake? He's going to be waddling up to the table."

"I expect so," said the guard.

"What'd this one do?" said Liz.

"Nothing," said the guard.

Liz handed me the ticket across the window to the kitchen. Then she turned back to the guard. "Come again?" she said.

"He's innocent," said the guard. "An unlucky sap who got caught in the system. I want that order done up perfect. It's about the only thing I can do for him now and I don't want it messed up."

Liz didn't say anything for a while. The only sound in the place was the bubbling of oil in the deep fryer.

"You hear all that, Bret?" she called back to me.

"I heard it," I said.

"Bret will do it all up right for you," said Liz. "For him. For Michael. You want something while you're waiting? A coffee?"

The guard said no, then took a seat in a booth by the window. He sat there taking up space like a stray dog you didn't want in your house.

Liz came back to the kitchen and stood beside me.

"What do you think?" she said.

"About what?"

"You think it's true? They're going to fry an innocent man?"

"They don't fry them," I said. "That's what we do. Nowadays they inject them with poison."

She hit my shoulder. "I'm serious," she said.

"So am I," I said. "If he is innocent, then we may as well give our all to this meal, like the guard said."

A couple came in the door. They glanced at the guard, who now looked like he was ready to cry, and quickly looked away. They fumbled for the door knob to leave. Liz walked over quickly and guided the couple across the floor to another booth where they couldn't see the guard. I needed to get his order out quick or he was going to ruin tonight's take.

I'm not a religious person, not by a long stretch. Liz has more in her along those lines than me, but not by much. Even so, as I rustled up that fish and those chips in the oil, I did begin to think about what I was doing. Giving nourishment to someone about to die. Granting a last request. I imagined I was like a holy man, performing a holy rite.

That was almost more unnerving than realizing he was probably innocent. Who was I to do this important thing? I wished the guard hadn't told us who the order was for.

Liz came back with another ticket. The couple wanted burgers: beef for him, chicken for her.

I took down six take-out boxes and put a container of coleslaw in each one, then a slice of bread next to it. The boxes were corrugated and molded so there were little compartments for everything. As the fries got done, I lifted them out of the oil and let the excess drip off while I started on the burgers for the couple. I had the grill and the fryers going, everything humming and sizzling along, just the way I like it.

Then the timer on the fish dinged and I pulled them out of the grease too.

Liz came back.

"That guard is about the saddest looking guy I've ever seen in my life," she said.

I nodded. "I'd be sad too if I thought some guy was getting killed who wasn't guilty."

"But how does he know?" said Liz. "That's what I'm wondering."

"Why don't you go ask him?" I said.

She turned red. "I couldn't."

"Sure you could."

"It's none of my business."

"Here," I said. "You fill up the boxes. I'll go ask him." I pulled off my apron, tossed it on the counter and walked through the swinging door, onto the floor, and over to the guard's booth. I sat down across from him. He barely noticed me, but after a couple of seconds he looked up.

"That order ready?" he said.

"Liz'll be out with it in a second. Can I ask you something?"

"No."

"Come on."

"I know what you want to ask me, but I can't tell you how I know. I just do."

"From being around him?"

The guard nodded. "That, and how the other inmates talk about him. Everyone in prison is innocent, know what I mean?"

I knew, but I didn't tell the guard how. I just nodded.

"They all say that," said the guard, "so after a while you learn to ignore it. But with him, it's different. All the other inmates believe him."

That didn't seem like much to go on. Maybe this guy was just a good liar. "You tell the warden?" I said. "The judge? His lawyer?"

"I told all of them what I know, which isn't much. Nothing that would mean anything in any court. Plus he's had all his appeals. Even the Supreme Court turned him down."

"Still. There must be something."

"His lawyers have a clemency request in, but no one's got any hope. The governor has never commuted a death sentence. He's not going to start now."

"You never know," I said.

The guard grunted.

"You're telling me," I said, "that you have a sixth sense about it. Is that right?"

The guard nodded. "I tell you what," he said. "This is tearing me up. I don't like when we kill the guilty ones. But this." He took off his cap and put it down on the table and ran his fingers through his hair. "I'm getting too soft for this. I can't spend time with them every day for months and years, then watch them shuffle off like this. Even the bad ones, you get to be friends with them, you know?"

"They become like family," I said.

He nodded. "Yup."

I thumped the table with both hands in a kind of drum roll. "I'll go get that order for you," I said.

He nodded.

I went back to the kitchen just as Liz was folding the lid over on the last box. "What'd you find out?" she said.

"Nothing."

"He clammed up?"

"No. He just doesn't know anything. Got a *feeling*."

"Don't sound so disgusted about it," she said. "Sometimes feelings are all we got to go on. You need to learn to trust yours."

She scooped up the boxes, stopped at the fridge to retrieve the cake, and went out on the floor to the guard's booth. As I finished up the burger orders, I watched the guard put his hat on and touch his forehead before taking the order. He offered to pay, but Liz wouldn't let him. We never let them pay for the last meals. Doesn't feel right to Liz. I don't get it myself. It's not coming from the guard's pocket. It's state money, but don't try to tell Liz that.

"Last meals are a gift," she told me once. "You don't take money for gifts."

The guard tried to insist, but Liz put up her hands and patted him on the shoulder. The guard looked like he was going to cry. I swear to God. But he didn't. He walked out the door holding the pile of boxes like they were Christmas packages and he was Santa Claus. A *sad* Santa, but nevertheless.

Liz came back with her eyes all wet and tears streaming down her face.

"I think he's right," she said. "The guy is completely innocent."

"Now how do you know that?" I said.

"I have a *feeling*," she said, and scooped up the plates with the burgers and took them to the couple in the booth.

I sighed, thinking I had said something wrong. I wasn't going to apologize, though, because I didn't know *what* I had said wrong.

The rest of the night passed quickly. Business picked up and we shot out orders like the whole town was getting ready to fast for a couple of weeks. By the time we closed up and cleaned up it was close to eleven o'clock. Liz hit the lights. "That poor guy is going to be dead in a little over an hour," she said.

I nodded. The only thing I wanted to do was go home, have a cold beer, maybe watch some stupid funny show on TV, then hit the sack. We stepped out into the night. The glow from the prison lit up the horizon like a small night light, showing the way to purgatory. It's always there at night, but on that evening, with what we knew—or thought we knew about the condemned guy— it was an irritating thing. It tried to crawl over from the horizon into my brain. Sounds crazy, but that's what it felt like. Like we had done something wrong.

We walked across the parking lot to our car, right where we had left it twelve hours ago when we opened for lunch.

"You're quiet," said Liz.

"Nothing much to say," I said.

"An innocent man is going to die tonight. Michael Rand is his name. Killed by the state. That kind of thing ever bother you?"

"Sure it bothers me," I said.

"I can't tell."

"What am I going to do about it?" I said. "I can't fix it."

"Not asking you to fix it," she said.

I got in the driver's seat. Liz sat beside me. We buckled our seat belts, the clicking noises a lot louder than I remembered from other times. I started the car. Wanted to turn on the radio, but it felt like this wasn't the time, so I backed out of the parking place and pulled onto the highway and started heading home. The silence between us felt like a fortification made of bricks and—something else. Resentment, maybe. Funny thing, I couldn't tell if it was hers or mine. We just both seemed to be different that night.

A couple of cars drove past us. Their headlights loomed bigger than full moons as they went by.

"I want to go there," said Liz.

Her voice startled me, like it made me wake up when I wasn't ready. "Go where?"

"To the execution."

That didn't sound like a good idea. They wouldn't let us in, for one thing. We could probably only get to the gate. And at the gate, there'd be people holding signs. Some wanting to see the guy killed, others wanting him alive. It was a sad old spectacle. We'd both seen it on the news many times.

"What do you want to go there for?" I asked.

"I don't know."

"Must be a reason," I said.

"Not everything needs a reason."

"It's late."

"I know it's late, Bret. I can tell the time."

I didn't turn around. Didn't slow down. Gave no indication that I was to going to do what she wanted me to do.

"If you don't want to take me," she said, "then just drop me off here. I'll walk there and find my way home. Maybe a nice anti-death-penalty activist will give me a ride."

"You forget," I said. "I used to live there."

Liz turned her eyes from the road ahead and looked at me. I didn't even know why this night was turning into a fight between us, but that was what it felt like. A strange fight.

"I don't forget," she said. "But I have to go there. Don't ask me why, because I don't understand it myself, but he's eaten my food. Our food."

I had been in prison once, for long enough that some of the despair got into my blood and I didn't want to revisit the sadness of the place. I got caught stealing cars. Lots of them. Got into a fight with some guys, too, and put a couple of them in the hospital. The state didn't care much for that kind of behavior, so they made me pay a debt to society.

I won't say prison made me a better man. It doesn't work that way. But after prison, I became better so I wouldn't go back there. That was about the time I met Liz and she decided she wanted to marry me. Always taking a chance on people, that was Liz. Always ready to believe the best in them could come out.

Turned out she was mostly right about me.

I slowed the car way down and circled at an intersection and accelerated as we got going in the opposite direction. My brain was calculating how much time this was going to take from us and how much sleep we weren't going to get and what that would do to our day tomorrow, starting at 10 again and going for all of lunch and supper. Liz snaked her hand across the seat and took mine and squeezed it. Just enough to let me know she wasn't doing this just for herself.

We got to the gate and it was like I expected, only more so. Must have been close to two hundred protestors. There was no way we were going to get close to the prison itself, although I wasn't at all sure that was what Liz wanted anyway.

I parked the car a couple hundred feet from the mass of sign wavers. I never had much use for protestors. They were entitled to their opinion, I guess, but what did I care about their opinions? I had opinions of my own, but I kept them to myself. Isn't that the way to better interpersonal relations? I like to think so.

Liz got out of the car and started walking to the group. I got out and trotted up behind her to catch up. She walked with what I recognized as her determined stride.

"You on a mission?" I asked.

"Something like that," she said.

"Care to let me in on it?"

"You wouldn't understand."

"Try me."

She kept walking, but she slowed her pace a little as we got close to a guy holding up a sign that said something about the state shouldn't be doing murder. Or maybe it was that you can't erase a murder with another murder. Or it could have been how the state was going to be shamed by history because it was killing an innocent man. Or was it that he didn't want the state committing murder in his name. Something. I don't remember, exactly.

"I want everyone to know I'm the one who fed him his last meal," said Liz.

"Why?"

"Bret, I can't explain it. I just have to do this."

She hurried her pace again. This time I didn't follow her. I didn't want to. For one thing, we were close to the prison and I never liked being close to that building. Made me feel all squinky in my gut, like something was trying to squeeze the juice right out of me from the inside out. So I stood there in the dark and the cold. Stars above looking down on me. The same stars looking down on the roof over the guy who was going to die soon. Michael Rand. They saw me standing and shivering. Maybe they saw him, too, if he had a window where he was. Poor guy was probably standing, maybe pacing. Maybe sitting down. But could be he was shivering too. From fright, not cold.

Liz walked right into the mass of people clustered around the gate. They parted for her. That determination she has, it's a universal signal: *don't get in my way.* She kept walking right up to the front of the group, where a guy stood on a box holding a megaphone. When he saw Liz, he stepped down and handed her the megaphone. Liz climbed up on the box and turned to face the group. Liz is a small woman. I could barely see the top of her head above the heads of the sign wavers.

Liz put the megaphone up to her mouth.

"My name is Liz," she said. "Me and my husband Bret own the diner down the road. You want a good meal, come by there anytime between eleven in the morning and nine at night."

Some laughter from the group.

"Why I'm here tonight," said Liz, "is that we made the last meal for the man that's about to die in the death chamber tonight."

Things got quiet, like they were already at a funeral. Liz didn't say anything for a few moments. The megaphone emitted some tiny electronic pops.

"My husband didn't want to bring me here tonight," said Liz. "But I came for a reason. See, when I was making his meal, I cried. Tears came out of me and I felt this sadness. The worst kind of sadness, because I knew something was being done that was wrong. But I couldn't fix it. Have you all felt that sadness?"

Murmurs of assent from everyone there. I hoped Liz wasn't going to point me out. Or tell people I had been a prisoner here once. I didn't want that recognition. Not tonight.

"But here's the thing," she said. "I forgot to pray over his food."

I blinked. This was why she came here?

"So I'm going to ask us all to pray for him. I'm going to ask us all to say grace over his last meal."

My wife Liz, she gets some crazy ideas in her head sometimes. I sure didn't think anyone there was going to pray with her, but I was wrong. Everyone instantly bowed their heads. Most of them lowered their signs so you couldn't read them.

And then Liz:

"We ask the almighty Earth, source of all abundance, keeper of oceans and forests, maker of deserts and mountains, we ask Earth to bless the food that Michael ate this evening and that it may fortify him for his passing."

That was it. A few lines. I had never heard them before from anyone, much less Liz. She held the megaphone for a few more seconds. I heard some sniffling in the group gathered around her. My own eyes seemed to be itching some. And my nose. I had to scratch it a couple of times.

Liz handed the megaphone back to the guy she got it from and stepped off the box and came back to me. I thought maybe we were going to hug each other, but that didn't happen. She caught my eye as she walked by me. I followed behind her until we got to the car and we both got into our seats, still warm from when we were in them only a few minutes before. I started the car.

"You get done what you wanted?" I asked.

"I did," said Liz.

We were still silent. Remained silent all the way home. But it was different this time. There was not a wall between us. Liz stared out the window. When the clock on the dashboard showed a big glowing numeral 12 with two zeros after it I think we both skipped a heart beat.

We got to our house a few minutes later and went inside. Neither of us wanted to go to bed. We clicked on the TV. Both of us, I think, were hoping some miracle had occurred and the governor had commuted the sentence. But that didn't happen. There was a short item near the end of the broadcast. They said Michael Brand had been executed as per the order of the warden at midnight.

"They didn't even get his name right," said Liz. She wasn't upset, not that I could tell. It was more a kind of wonder at the thought. How could someone not even know the real name of the dead?

"I'm sorry," I said. And I was. For Liz.

"I am too," she said. "I never want to make one of those meals again."

"Next time they come to us, we'll just say no," I said.

Liz slid across the couch closer to me. "I never even knew him," she said.

"I know."

"But I feel like he was part of our family. We made food for him."

I had no words for her. I think I wanted to stop thinking about Michael Rand. About his crime. About him being where I used to live.

The next morning neither of us wanted to go to work, but we did. We drove into our diner and opened it up and started prepping and soon the crowds came in for lunch and we got lost in the whirl of it all. Michael Rand shrunk to a tiny piece of our awareness.

A week later, towards the middle-of-the-day lull, I turned on the radio and listened to the news. No mention of Michael Rand, of course, but there was one little bit of news that made us shiver.

Seems the governor had a change of heart and had decided to commute all the death sentences of all the inmates in all the prisons in the state to life without possibility of parole. He wasn't the first. Other governors had done the same. But it was a surprise in our state, where most people believed in the death penalty pretty strongly.

I heard that news with a mixture of despair and astonishment. Surely some that deserved to die were now not going to. But on the other hand, there were almost certainly some in that group who didn't deserve to die and now they weren't going to. I glanced over at Liz, who was busy rearranging stuff in the fridge.

"Did you hear that, Liz?" I said. "Did you hear that? No more executions. No more last meals. You were right. We won't have to do anymore of them."

And Liz, she didn't turn around to look at me or look up at the sky or even pause in her moving stuff around. The only thing I noticed was that she moved a jar of pickles about six times. From one place to another and then back to the original place and then back to the other place. She did this for a long time, until she got tired of it, I guess, and then she stood with the fridge door open and her hand trembling on the handle, like she sometimes did when she tried lifting something that turned out to be too heavy and she had to ask me to help her with it.

Salmon Don't Foretell the Future

THE AIR HUNG still and quiet and a mist settled into the Columbia River Gorge and filled up my little town perched on the shore of the big river like a drab pebble. The moon above me looked like an over-boiled potato, the extremities of it undefined and murky.

Judge Mary Davis, my old high school friend, required my presence at her house. She had called me at home earlier in the day. I didn't know what she wanted. Not exactly. I had an idea I wouldn't like it. I had a particular talent: I could sometimes see the future. Not all the time, but enough that Mary could find some use for it. She almost certainly planned to appeal to my sense of justice.

Cunning of her.

Maybe I wasn't going to fall for it.

I stood on the pedestrian bridge over Rock Creek and watched the moon's smudge reflected in the water: a dozen white crescents jumped spasmodically in the ripples. They tried to coalesce into a coherent image, but failed miserably. Their futile dance suited my melancholy mood. I was a middle-aged man, never married, no grandchildren—hell, no *children*—and no prospects for companionship or tribal ties. Never been in love. Why shouldn't I be melancholy?

Fall had turned the air cold and crisped up the leaves. Many of them littered the bridge. I took some pleasure in stepping on those leaves and hearing the crunch, like collapsing insect shells. Recent rains had swelled the creek enough to make the water chortle as it passed over the rocks. I normally didn't identify with a happy sound, so I let it flow through and out of me without snagging any of it.

Dark shapes moved in the water: some raggedy salmon had found their way into the creek from the Columbia and fought the current with their super salmon will, just so they could get to their dying spot upstream that much sooner.

I got to the judge's house about a quarter after eight. She had one of the nicer houses in town. A judge's salary can do that for a person. The grass in the yard looked like a barber had trimmed it that afternoon. Soft flood lights lit the brick exterior so the house glowed in the night.

I stepped up to the front door and rang the doorbell. Of course it worked, unlike mine, which had been broken for I can't remember how many years.

Judge Davis answered the door.

"Peter," she said. "Thanks for coming."

She invited me inside. Some cop show played on the television.

"Can I get you anything?" she said.

"I've eaten," I said.

"Then let's go to my office."

I followed her upstairs to what the house's designers intended to be one of the bedrooms. Mary's kids were long grown and moved out and she and her husband had divorced years ago. The bedroom now held a big wooden desk surrounded by shelves supporting thick legal books, all lined up like toy soldiers and all wearing the same uniform: a dark blue, like someone had taken the sky, roasted it on an open fire to give it a meaty texture and wrapped pieces of it around bound pages.

Judge Davis loved her legal books. I could tell by the way she showcased them. I imagined she liked having them look down on her. Maybe they made her want to do her job better.

She indicated a chair in front of the desk and I flopped into it. One of those roller chairs. Kind of flimsy feeling. I noticed she had a much plusher chair behind her desk: thick arm rests and padded back. Brown leather. It suited her.

"So what can I do for you?" I asked.

She took a file from a corner of the desk and slid it toward me. Thin. Looked like it held only a few pages. I picked it up and opened it.

The picture on the first page looked like a kid. That surprised me. Mary presided over a criminal court. They usually don't get juveniles. I glanced up at Mary. Her face betrayed no expression. She just studied me.

Fine.

I went back to the file. It *was* a kid. Fifteen years old. A long list of priors, mostly burglaries and assaults. Fifteen. I looked at the birth date again, to be sure. I shook my head. A career criminal at so young an age. It hardly seemed logistically possible. Now he was up for a sexual assault. He had broken into a house to burglarize it and while he was at it he raped the 72 year old woman who lived there.

The evidence looked completely damning. I put the folder back on Mary's desk and asked the question anyway.

"Is he guilty?"

"As sin."

"So what do you need from me?"

"I have a choice. I can sentence him to life without parole, or I can give him something lesser. Something that will maybe let him out in fifteen or twenty years."

"When he's become a young man with the capacity for moral choice, which he clearly lacks now?"

"Exactly," said Mary.

"He's a monster," I said.

"He's also a child. He might change. He could grow out of being a monster. We shouldn't give up on children if there's a chance. Only I can't tell if he'll change. You can."

Of course. That's why I was sitting in front of her, reading about a monster.

"Is the victim okay?"

"That's not important to this discussion."

"It is to me."

"Why? It doesn't change what you can do for me."

That legal mind. She got to the heart of things and nothing else mattered.

She was the same in high school: worked hard, straight As, always knew what mattered and what didn't.

The last day of high school, we sat together in the cafeteria at one of the tables. The odor of grease heavy in the air. I wasn't going to miss that nauseating smell. Mary was about to go off to college, eventually to law school. I knew she would succeed. I was destined to stay in town, get a job in the administration department at the school district, away from people, and stick with it for a few decades. We had a copy of the yearbook between us and we sat flipping through it. A sad mood clung to us, like we were looking at people we might not ever see again, and something in me, I don't know what, made me start passing judgement on each one. Sort of a roundup of who was most likely to succeed.

Or not.

"This one is going to make it," I said, pointing to the picture of the nerdiest kid in school.

"No way," said Mary.

"Oh yeah," I said. "And this one—" I flipped to a photo of the quarterback "—will crash and burn before he's twenty-five. Drugs."

"That's ridiculous. How can you know that?"

I shrugged. "I just know," I said. "That one will die of cancer in her forties. This one will invent a device that every car in the world will use and he'll be richer than anyone. That one gets divorced three times and never finds happiness. This one will be a pervert and spend years in jail."

And so on. I went through the whole book. I don't know where the judgements came from, they were simply there, on the tip of my tongue as I looked at each photo and the person rose up into my consciousness.

I had no idea at the time that I was right. I mostly forgot the whole episode, because it was a stupid thing, a crazy lark. Something to pass the time at the end of my high school career. A joke, really, nothing more.

Only Mary remembered. She had that kind of mind. She kept each judgement folded into her brain. Then, years later, when some of my predictions started coming true, she contacted me.

"Peter," she said on the phone. "This is Mary Davis. Remember me?"

By that time our lives had diverged. She had become a prosecuting attorney in Portland, forty miles away, several worlds removed from my realm.

"Mary. Sure. How have you been?"

"I'm fine. Did you hear about Alex?"

"Alex?"

"You remember. The football player at our school. The quarterback."

"Sure," I said.

"He died of an overdose."

He died of an overdose. "I didn't know that," I said. Why would I? Alex moved from town right after he graduated. Last I heard he got some kind of scholarship to a school in Florida. That was a long time ago.

"It's exactly like you predicted," said Mary.

At first I didn't know what she meant by that, and then I remembered the incident with the yearbook. I *did* say something about him getting into drugs. I did *know*, didn't I?

"And that other guy, the one you said was going to be a pervert?"

"Tom."

"Yeah, Tom. He was arrested a few weeks ago for sex with a ten year old. Stone cold pervert. Exactly like you said."

The phone felt heavy in my hand. A cold sweat broke out on my forehead and I wanted to hang up on Mary. All the judgements I had made on my school mates came back to me, swirling in my brain. I didn't need to know this. Didn't need to know any of this. I had no power. This made no sense.

"Peter?" said Mary. "You have a gift. We should find a way to use it."

So simple for her. So straightforward. Mary had been through law school. You'd think that would expunge any mumbo jumbo woo woo notions right out of anyone's brain. Not Mary's. She saw something that worked and accepted it without question. She just needed to find a way to make it work for her.

Those memories came flooding back to me as I sat across from her desk, three decades after leafing through the yearbook.

"We had a deal," said Mary. "Remember?"

"I remember," I said quietly.

Mary did a favor for me. When she had been a prosecutor, just before she became a judge, she pulled a few strings and got a charge against me dismissed. It was a hit and run. I won't try to justify myself. It happened a long time ago on a particularly stormy night. Wind lashed rain against my car as I drove down I-84. I learned later that the person I hit had broken down and was parked on the shoulder, chose not to stay with her car. Instead, she got out and edged over to the side of the oncoming lane and tried to flag someone down for help. With the water spraying everywhere in front of my face, my windshield wipers going like crazy not clearing my view completely, I wandered over the line onto the shoulder.

I never saw her.

I felt something. A shudder go through the car. I should have stopped, but it felt too dangerous. I told myself I ran over some road debris, even though it didn't feel like that at all. It felt like nothing I had ever experienced driving a car.

The woman died. The cops caught up with me. The charge was vehicular manslaughter and leaving the scene of a crime. Serious stuff. I had a lawyer. He told me, given the charge, I would probably be doing some kind of time. I accepted his assessment. What choice did I have? Then, at the last minute, my problem got reduced to a misdemeanor. I had to pay a fine and I was done. My lawyer was stunned.

"How did that happen?" he asked me, completely mystified. Me. Like I knew anything.

Mary called me a few days later.

"Peter?" she said.

"Mary?"

"How are you enjoying your freedom?"

Then it came clear to me. My old high school friend used her pull to take care of me. I felt like I should thank her. Something in her voice made me think she wanted more than gratitude.

"It was you, then," I said. "It was you who fixed things for me." The mystery cleared, I no longer felt euphoria. It was more a sickness in the pit of my stomach.

"No need to discuss that," she said. "These sorts of things happen. The wheels of justice, and so on."

"And so on," I said.

"What I'm calling about is to let you know I may need to call on your abilities at some time in the future."

"My abilities."

"You know what I mean. I hope your gratitude will allow you to see your way clear to helping me out."

I didn't say anything. Her comments sounded sinister to my ear, and I couldn't even tell why.

"I can't help you tell what really happened to someone," I said. "If that's what you're thinking."

"You mean you can't tell if someone is lying or not, is that what you're saying?"

"Yes, Mary. That's what I'm saying." After some of my predictions with my classmates began panning out, I retreated from the world. Kept myself away from people. I had discovered that physical contact with a person, even for a moment, allowed me to see their future. Like with the kids in the yearbook. I had known all those people when I was in high school, had been next to each one, had brushed against them in the hall, or at some other point had touched them, even if only very briefly.

That kind of knowledge scared me. I didn't want any part of it. The intimacy was too overpowering. So I retreated into myself.

"That's not what I want from you," she said.

"Okay," I said. "Then I'm confused."

"How does it work?"

"How does what work?"

"You know what I'm asking. How do you see into people's future?"

"I have to touch them," I said.

"Ahhh," she said, like I told her something she had suspected. Now she had confirmation.

"I'm still confused about what you want from me." I said.

"Don't be. Just enjoy your life. I'll call you if I need you."

Then she hung up.

Not exactly the phone call from someone who wants to rekindle an old friendship. More a threat. "Enjoy your life." Sure, if my life could be enjoyed.

Mine had some deficiencies in that regard. It's no fun getting to know people when even the briefest and most glancing of intimacies leads to the knowledge of that person's future. When they will die.

So I worked hard to make sure I never had that knowledge. I stayed away from people as much as possible. I had a reputation as a loner. I was, in fact, one of the town eccentrics.

Years went by. Mary never called on me. I knew she still lived in town. Had moved to the heights, where the lots were bigger and the other houses were huge and imposing so the one she had built fit right in. I also knew she became a criminal court judge in Portland. She made the hour commute back and forth everyday.

Her career was going along nice and smooth. On my rare trips into town I would see her and she would see me and we would nod at each other and that was it. I assumed, naively, that she had forgotten about me and my ability.

I was wrong. She was biding her time. She wanted me to tell her what the future of the child monster held.

"What exactly are you asking me to do?" I said.

"The jury's already found him guilty. That was the easy part. Tomorrow come the arguments from the lawyers. That's not going to be so easy. They know I have a choice. The defense guy is going to argue that he's a baby and he can't get life without parole. The prosecutor will say the kid acted like an adult so he should be punished like an adult. It's all up to me. I don't want to make the wrong decision. And in this case, there is a right decision, it depends on his destiny. If he changes, then he should have the possibility of parole. If he will not, if he will remain a detestable being with no sense of morality or natural constraint on his violent tendencies, then I will feel perfectly justified in giving him life without possibility of parole."

I saw her dilemma. I also saw why she wanted me to help her out. No one else on the planet could help her at this point.

"I don't want to touch this kid," I said. Simple as that.

"I haven't asked for that favor up to now," said Mary.

"I know."

"When was that, when you had that stroke of luck and got off with a slap on the wrist?"

I thought back. "Must be twenty years now."

"Twenty years. If fortune hadn't smiled on you, much of those twenty years would have been spent in jail. Ever think of that?"

"Mostly I think about that poor woman. Sometimes I think how stupid she was, wandering around an interstate highway like that in the rain at night. Mostly I feel bad for her. I tell myself it wasn't my fault. Not really. I don't always convince myself."

"Sounds like you've begun to feel sorry for yourself. Is that it, Peter?"

"There's a lot to regret. I never should have gone through that yearbook. At least not with you sitting beside me."

"You know I remember every prediction. I've followed our classmates. You've been right every time."

"I feel no joy about that," I said.

"Only sadness?"

I nodded.

"I never understood you," she said. "You have this amazing gift and you have chosen to deny it. Do you know how far you could have gone if you had used it?"

She was asking me why I didn't have the courage to embrace who I was. I had no answer for her. The world is full of pain. People carry an enormous load of it with them. All the time. You tap into too much of that, and you have a hard time conducting a life of your own.

Judge Mary Davis drummed her desk impatiently with her finger tips.

"It's simple," she said. "Come to the courthouse tomorrow. *My* courthouse. I'll arrange for you to have contact with the defendant. Later I'll ask you what you got from him."

I didn't want to oblige her. I didn't need to see into the mind of a monster.

"Remember," she said. "Sometimes fortune can go the other way."

ON THE WAY home I stopped at the grocery store to pick up a few items. I paid with a check, and laid it down on the counter. I always paid with a check. With cash, you got change back and sometimes you ended up touching the hand of the checker when she put the change in your palm. That didn't happen if you put the check down on the counter. People in town were used to my little eccentricities. They thought I was OCD. Which was fine. It worked out for me and for them that way.

At home, getting ready for bed, I wondered how much I really owed Mary. Sure, she had helped me through a sticky situation, ages ago. Why was she calling in that favor now? Something about this case really troubled her. Such a young kid, doing such horrible things. You didn't want to guess wrong. Unfortunately, as a judge, she didn't have the power to see the future.

I did.

I hated that. I didn't want my ability. I kept it as quiet as I possibly could. So quiet only two people in the world knew about it. Me and Mary.

THE NEXT MORNING I drove into Portland and parked near the criminal courthouse. I went inside. They passed a wand over me, then let me through. I went up the stairs to the third floor. I got to Mary's door and stopped. I put up my hand and was ready to knock.

I hesitated.

I could still walk away.

Like I had walked that time I hit the woman. A lot of guilt there. Still. Felt it everyday. Maybe this was a way to get rid of it. Maybe Mary was doing me a favor, as well as herself.

Maybe.

I knocked on the door and stepped inside. Her clerk took me through the front room to the back and showed me into Judge Davis's inner office, then left me there, alone.

Mary showed up a few seconds later. "Ahh," she said. "You decided to come. I wasn't sure you would."

"No," I said. "You don't have that power. I do."

She looked funny in her robes. They made her look like a statue, the way they curved and hung like bronze.

She studied me for a few seconds. No expression on her face. I imagined she felt pity for me, the way I squandered my God given ability.

"You never told me about me," she said.

"You?"

"You had a story for everyone in the yearbook except me."

"I couldn't tell you."

"Why not?"

"It didn't seem right, to tell you right to your face. The other kids, none of them were there. I never told a single one what I knew about them."

"I didn't want to ask about me," said Mary. "Not then."

I nodded.

"You've had this knowledge about me all these years."

"It's no big deal."

"Should I ask you what you know about me?"

"Up to you."

"And up to you if you tell me."

"That's right."

"Most of us don't have that knowledge of other people. Maybe there's a reason for it."

"I wouldn't be surprised," I said.

What I knew about Mary was that she was going to live a long time. Longer than my abilities could reach. Once someone got to about age 85, I couldn't tell any more. It was like they pulled away from my reach and entered some secondary world that I had no access to. Mary was one of those. Her life was going to chug along like the little engine that could right into her late eighties at least. I also didn't want to tell her because I didn't want her to know that my ability had some restrictions on it. I wanted her to think of me as more powerful than I really was.

"It bothers me that I will never know for sure what you think."

I shrugged. "That isn't why you asked me here today. Or is it?"

"No, of course not. He'll be here in a few minutes. I've asked his lawyer to bring him in on the pretext that I want to interview him to get to know him a little better."

"How do you stand it?" I asked.

"What?"

"Being around such horrible people."

"They're just people," she said.

"People who rape and maim."

"Don't think about that."

"How can I not?"

"You learn to be objective. He's a case like any other. I have to make an unbiased decision."

She must have known that I could not do the same thing. The fifteen-year-old was not just a kid. He was a hardened criminal.

Mary's clerk tapped on the door and pushed it open. "They're here," she said.

"Send them in," said Mary.

I looked at her. She avoided my eyes and looked past me to the door. I heard chains shuffle along the floor, then the boy entered. He didn't look anything like what I had expected. Cuffs locked his wrists together. He had an angelic face, smooth and radiant, like he had taken on the sun. And he smiled, like he was happy to be alive. And maybe he was. Maybe he liked being a criminal. Maybe that was his calling. I shook my head. Horrible thought.

Was I interested in where he was going to end up? No. I didn't want to know. I especially didn't want to know if he was going to become even worse than he was now. Mary could sentence him to death for all I cared.

A guard and a guy in a suit, someone I took to be his lawyer, stood on either side of him. The suit spoke first. "Judge, may I ask what this is about?"

"Indulge me, please," said Mary. "I want your client to shake hands with my friend."

"Excuse me?" said the suit.

"A simple thing. You think your client could oblige me?"

"I don't see what this will accomplish."

"I need it for my appraisal. I need it to make a decision about my sentence."

The kid had a suspicious look to him. Truth to tell, the guard had a similar look. This had to be out of the ordinary.

"Peter," said Mary, "meet David."

David didn't put his hand up. His lawyer nudged him, hard enough that the kid had to shuffle his feet a little to catch his balance. Not so easy in those chains. All I could think about was his victim, that 72-year-old woman. I wanted to hand her a gun and have her shoot the kid. Might do everyone some good. The kid looked up at me and smiled. I wanted to see evil in his eye, I didn't. Damn it. That wasn't right. He was a monster, wasn't he?

His cuffs tinkled as he lifted his arms and extended one hand toward me.

Now it was my turn. I felt a pressure on my hand. It wanted to lift itself, I wouldn't let it.

"Peter?" said Mary.

David's smile held for several seconds. Soon the ends of his mouth started to tremble. His lips began to change to a sneer. His lawyer looked at Mary, appealing to her sense of—what? I wasn't sure. I don't think the lawyer was either.

"Fuck this," said David. He spat on the floor. "Fuck you," he said to me.

He dropped his hand.

Mary looked at me with pity in her eyes. Then she moved, quicker than I would have imagined. She came from around her desk, grabbed my arm, and pushed it onto David's head. David tried to duck away. He couldn't move fast enough.

I felt revulsion as my palm passed over his hair. I thought I might be sick all over Mary's carpet. Mary held my hand on David's head for too long. It seemed like hours. David stopped trying to move away.

"Your honor," said David's lawyer. "Please explain what you're doing here."

I was expecting to see horrible things. Awful visions of what David was destined for. Instead, I saw—

—nothing.

What the—?

Mary released my hand. I pulled it away from David, reluctantly. There was nothing. No knowledge in the touch. No future vision. Nothing to tell if this kid was going to be anything evil or angelic.

It appeared my powers had gone away.

I looked at Mary and shook my head. She understood immediately. I saw the air go out of her.

She dismissed David and his lawyer. The suit looked exceedingly perplexed as he followed the guard and his client out the door. Presumably he was going to the courthouse to await his sentencing. And what was that sentence going to be?

That was up to Mary.

"When did it disappear?" she asked me quietly.

"I don't know," I said. "I've avoided contact with people for years. It must have quit on me when I wasn't looking."

"There's nothing left?"

"No."

"Then I waited too long."

"Looks that way."

She retreated to her chair and sat down in it glumly. Her robes no longer looked so regal. They looked more like a pile of rags gathered up on her lap.

"I'm back where I started."

"Use your judgement, like you always did. I bet it's served you well."

She sighed. "I've made some mistakes. Been merciful when I shouldn't have. Been tougher than necessary other times."

"Surely that's an occupational hazard," I said.

"This one was important."

"Why this one so much?"

"I hate throwing away children."

I could understand that. I couldn't help her. The only thing I wanted then was to leave the courtroom and go hug someone. Anyone. I wanted the blissful joy of not knowing anything about them, even after I touched them.

She stood up. "Thanks for coming," she said.

"You didn't give me much choice."

"You didn't take my subtle threats seriously, did you?"

"Um. No. Of course not. Well, maybe a little."

"What's the worst thing you did when you were fifteen?"

It seemed a strange question. "I stole some candy from a convenience store."

"Candy?"

"Yeah. Didn't even like it."

"Then why did you do it?"

"Coming from a judge, who's seen it all, that's a strange question."

"I suppose." She came around and stood in front of me. "They're waiting for me. I have to be the wise one now."

"What are you going to decide?"

She moved slowly. Made me think of the salmon, crawling against the current in Rock Creek, trying to fight the forces, making such slow ground. They ground out their lives as best they could. They never saw the future. Never knew what awaited them.

She put out her hand. I took it.

"I wonder if maybe we can be friends again. If that's okay with you."

Contact with her hand brought no knowledge of any kind. I was happier than I had ever been in my life.

"That would be fine with me," I said.

The Visitor From the Dark Mountain

ALICIA AND HER husband Karl lived off the grid in the woods near Mount Hood in the Cascade Range of northern Oregon. They had a house of stone they built themselves and some adjoining land where they grew their own food and lived a simple life away from much of civilization.

One day, late in the summer, Alicia was harvesting honey from the bees she and Karl kept in wooden hives. They used some of the honey for themselves, but most of it was for trading with other independent and resourceful people like themselves. Karl was, that very day, at a neighbor's farm trading honey for an old pickup truck.

A man came down the road and saw Alicia bent over the bees. He surveyed her house and noted its superior workmanship. The house not only looked sturdy and tough, it was also neat and attractive. Not that it was a mansion, by any means, or even a fine building fit for a well-to-do family. It was, however, a solid structure, the sort of house thrifty and hard-working people would have. This pleased the man.

"Hello there," he called to Alicia.

Alicia stood up from her bees, took off her netted head gear, and turned around. As soon as she saw the man she smiled widely. "Hello, sir," she said. "I don't believe I know you."

"I'm not from here," said the man. "I'm visiting from the dark mountain."

"The dark mountain, you say?" said Alicia.

"Yes, I've been traveling a long time. I would appreciate a small bite to eat if you can spare it."

Alicia and Karl knew enough to be wary of strangers, but they were also generous people, willing to help others in need.

"Please come inside," said Alicia.

"Thank you," said the man.

"What is your name?" said Alicia.

"I am called Ivan."

"Ivan," said Alicia. "What a grand name. Come, come."

Alicia walked with Ivan up the path to her front door. They stepped inside and Alicia invited Ivan to sit at the kitchen table. Ivan pulled out a chair and made himself comfortable. Alicia brought him a glass of water and put a plate of stew in front of him. Ivan dug in happily and grinned when Alicia handed him a crusty piece of bread that he dipped into the stew.

"This is very good," he said. "Thank you so much."

"It's nothing," said Alicia. "Tell me a little about the dark mountain."

"What would you like to know?" said Ivan.

"My mother died about a year ago," said Alicia. "Do you know her on the dark mountain?"

"Maybe," said Ivan. "I know a lot of people on the dark mountain. What's her name?"

"Nadine."

"Oh, sure," said Ivan. "I know her."

"Really?" said Alicia.

Ivan glanced at Alicia's hair and face. "Of course," he said. "White hair and high cheekbones. Brown eyes."

"That's her!" said Alicia. She pulled out a chair for herself and sat down next to Ivan. "How's she doing on the dark mountain?"

Ivan took another bite of his bread. "Well," he said. "I don't want to be the one to tell you, but your poor mother is not doing so good at all."

Alicia's face fell. "Oh no," she said.

Ivan nodded. "It's sad. She has no honey, you see, so when people come over to visit, she has nothing for them. Without honey she can't make any treats. And she has no sweetener for tea. She is so embarrassed that she doesn't have people over anymore at all."

"That's terrible," said Alicia. "My mother loves to have people over to her house."

"I know," said Ivan. "That's what makes it so sad."

"Are you going back to the dark mountain?" said Alicia.

"No," said Ivan, "I wasn't planning to for a while."

"Oh," said Alicia.

"Why do you ask?" said Ivan.

"I was thinking. If I gave you some honey, could you take it to my mother on the dark mountain so she can make treats for her guests?"

"I don't know about that," said Ivan. "It's a long way to the dark mountain. It's a lot of work getting back there."

"Oh, please," said Alicia. "I want to help my mother, but I can't go to the dark mountain on my own."

"Hmmm," said Ivan. "I can see you care about your mother." He tapped his finger on the table. "And you *did* give me a nice meal." He studied Alicia carefully. "Okay," he finally said. "Since you are such a nice lady, I will do this for you."

"That is wonderful!" said Alicia. "How much honey should I give you?"

"Well," said Ivan, "now that I think about it a little more, it will be hard for me to take a jar of honey big enough to last your mother for a long time. It would be so heavy. I think what would maybe be better is that you give me some money that I can take to your mother on the dark mountain and then she can buy the honey she needs."

Alicia thought about this and decided it made good sense. "Wait here," she said "and I will get you some money. How much do you think she will need?"

"How much do you have?" said Ivan. "I will be happy to give her as much as you think she needs."

Alicia went to the bedroom and reached under the mattress where her husband Karl had stored away some cash for emergencies. She pulled it all out and brought it to Ivan. "Will this help my mother?" she said.

"Oh, I do think so," said Ivan. He took the money and put it into his pocket. "Your mother is very lucky to have such a wonderful daughter as you."

"We're both lucky to have someone like you to help us."

"I'm only too happy to be of service," said Ivan.

Alicia showed him out the door and soon Ivan was on his way.

Alicia returned to her bees with a light heart. How often do you get a chance to help your own mother after she has died? Not very often at all, Alicia was sure of it.

A couple of hours later Alicia's husband Karl returned in the pickup truck he had acquired in trade for several dozen jars of honey. The truck was old and battered, but its engine hummed nicely. It was a good vehicle. Karl got out of the truck.

"Wow," said Alicia. "Looks like you got a bargain."

"Yup," said Karl. "I think I did okay."

"You sure did. Now let me tell you about the bargain I made today." Alicia began to tell Karl about her visit with Ivan, the man from the dark mountain.

Karl's face grew darker and darker as Alicia continued her story. When she was finished he had only one question.

"Where did this Ivan character go?"

Alicia pointed down the road.

Karl got back into his truck and took off after Ivan. It wasn't long before he saw the man, walking briskly along the road. Karl pressed down on the accelerator to catch up to him more quickly. Ivan heard the pickup and ran off the road into the woods. Karl parked the truck at the side of the road and quickly got out and ran into the woods himself, intending to catch Ivan and give him a good throttling for taking advantage of his wife and stealing their money.

But Ivan was quicker and more sly than Karl. He waited behind a tree as Karl ran by. When Karl was far enough into the woods, Ivan went back to the road, saw that the truck still had its key in the ignition, got into the truck, and drove away.

Karl heard the sound of tires on gravel. He hurried to where he left his truck but he was much too late. Ivan was already far down the road.

Karl stood on the shoulder. He watched his money and his new truck recede into the distance.

Wearily he trudged back to his house. Alicia was waiting for him.

"Where did you go in such a hurry?" she said. "And what happened to the truck?"

"You know that guy, Ivan, who is taking money to your mother?" he asked.

"Yes," said Alicia. "Did you catch up to him to thank him?"

Karl nodded. "Yes I did," he said. "I also talked him into taking our new truck to your mother to help her get around on the dark mountain."

"Oh," said Alicia. "That is wonderful! He is such a generous man."

"Yes," said Karl. "This Ivan character is quite an amazing fellow."

Assisted Living

PEOPLE ALWAYS SAY confession is good for the soul. What I always wondered is: whose soul? The confessor's? Not always. Sometimes the confessor ends up in prison for his troubles and no one can tell me prison is good for anyone's soul.

I'm 92 years old. Where I'm living now feels like a prison. Assisted living facility, they call it. More like assisted suicide if you ask me. Not that anyone asks me anything anymore.

I try talking to the other inmates—uh, excuse me, *residents*— but they don't want to hear it either. Stories. They get old after a while and end up the same as anyone else's: I grew up, I had some bad times, some good times, got laid, got married, got a job, got old, got tossed aside, and my kids don't want anything to do with me. So what else is new?

I spend a lot of my time in the great room where they have a TV and a fireplace. View of the cove through the window. Placid water, some ducks, a few swans in the winter. They fly north come spring. The Columbia River beyond that. Sailboarders skimming back and forth across it like butterflies in the wind. Butterflies die too, within a few days. They aren't pretty for long, that's for sure. Moldering on the ground in no time.

I'm on the Washington side of the river. Small town a couple of hours drive from Portland, Oregon. We don't have much here: a few hotels, some struggling businesses downtown. It's an old village, really, boom years long gone, back when the lumber industry was going full on cutting down trees like they were weeds.

Green cliffs of Oregon beyond the river. There's a world out there, but it's too big for my life now. This facility is just my size. It's all I can do to walk the length of it once or twice a day.

The swans on the cove are bigger than you think is possible for them to fly. They float around on the water like toys. Sometimes stick their heads down, butts in the air, looking for roots or something in the muck.

At least that's what a guy from the forest service said when he came to talk to us one day. Told us all about the habits of water fowl, like any of us cared. The people that run this place think we got nothing better to do while we're waiting to die than listen to blowhards go on about their obsessions.

Most of us let our obsession crumble a long time ago. Hobbies turn stale, that's one thing you learn after nine-plus decades of life. *Doing* becomes a chore. Most of us we just want to sit and eat.

I got a friend here. He can't remember nothing. Can't remember his *name*. Or the fact that he's married. His wife has her own room here. They meet every day and his wife tells him that he's her husband and he says No kidding? How about that? Then he smiles. He's got crazy teeth. All angled every which way so he looks like maybe he's been put together out of left over bricks, the ones that get broke on construction sites.

His wife always laughs and says they have kids. And even grandkids. And my friend just lights up when he hears this. It's like he's being given a brand new life. Maybe he has. I don't know. He got knocked in the head fifty years ago in the woods. Ever since then, he can't remember nothing.

That's a good way to be, I think. Have a tree fall on you, then be happy the rest of your life. People that remember things, it's a lot harder for them to be happy. A lot harder.

I told that to the gal who comes over with the books from the library. She's a nice girl. Listens to what we want. A lot of us, we like to read to pass the time, but getting to the library isn't so easy, so the librarian, she thought, why not bring the books to us? She carries over a couple of boxes of them and we get to pick out one or two.

At first it was all nice stuff she brought. You know, like *sweet* stories. Religious. Stories about dogs. Books that were supposed to make you *feel* good. She must have thought we didn't want to think about death. None of us residents cared anything about a single one of those books. The library gal was mystified so I told her most people here know those *nice* stories are a load of B.S. You want your books to circulate, I said, bring us murder stories. The bloodier the better.

Well, you'd have thought I told her we roasted babies alive and ate them with mint sauce every Sunday, the way she looked at me. I said, One thing you got to understand is we all aren't afraid of death for the most part. It makes us laugh if we even think about it at all.

So the next time she came she had a pile of gory murder books, some serial killer novels, a few Ann Rule books, things of that nature. They all got snapped up from her little library cart like we were buzzards picking road kill clean. Made her eyes go wide. I chuckled. Surprised? I asked her.

A little bit, she said. I had no idea.

Didn't think I knew what I was talking about, did you? I said. But I did. I did know.

As I said that to her I was aware of my voice breaking a little. I was close to tears. Nothing more pathetic than an old man crying. I hated that. Turned my eyes away from her then. People think when you get old you don't know anything. They want to dismiss you. I wanted her to know I wasn't dismissible, but I wasn't expecting it would make me want to cry.

She must have thought I was pathetic, but she didn't show it, which made me like her even more.

Do you like reading about gruesome murders, too? she asked.

With me, I said, it's personal. I committed a gruesome murder once. When I was about your age. Maybe 70 years ago.

I don't know what made me tell her. I had never told anyone else. There were only two other guys who knew about it and that was only because they participated. Okay, that's not quite exactly true. I did tell it to my friend, the one who forgets, but he doesn't know about it, since he forgot I told him.

The guys who did the killing with me, they both died a long time ago. So maybe I was feeling the burden of that lone knowledge and I needed to unload. Had to pass it on to the next generation. Mostly I think it was that the library gal seemed to be so nice to me. Seemed to want to know about me. Probably nothing more important to know about me than that one fact of my crime.

She barely reacted when I told her. It was like I had mentioned how the sun seemed to be shining pleasantly in the sky that afternoon.

I didn't elaborate on my crime. Didn't feel like I needed to.

Then, finally, she asked, You mean in the war?

I wondered which war she thought I had been in. I saw she was giving me an out, a way to save face. To hide the truth again.

No, I said. Not the war. The man we killed—me and my accomplices—did nothing to us. We were not soldiers. It was not self-defense. He was no threat to me or anyone else. It wasn't an accident. I helped kill him because I wanted to.

Her face went pale. A silence—like the kind that occurs between hymns at church, when echoes punctuate the air with soft clicks and distant taps—that was the omen-filled silence that fell upon us then. She stared at me and held my gaze and I stared right back.

We weren't born old, I said. None of us here were. We all had a life before this. With good things and bad. Do you want to hear more?

She did not. She made that very clear by the way she backed away from me and began gathering up the few books that no one had claimed, putting them into her box and getting ready to go. I thought to tell her I was only joking, but it was the most peculiar thing: I was glad I told her about my crime. Glad to have someone else carry the knowledge. I felt exactly like I was passing on a family secret to someone who would pass it on in her time.

Then I thought I might have made the biggest mistake of my life. What if she went to the police and told them what the guy at Assisted Living told her? What if the police came to my room one day and hauled me off?

Those first two or three days after I talked to her, I jumped at every sound, thinking the law was about to swoop down on me. Don't think I was ready to pay for my crime. I wasn't. I had gotten away with murder for close on three quarters of a century. I wasn't keen on breaking my streak. Not by a long shot.

You can think of me as a crazy old man. I won't argue with you too much on that point. Everyone gets a little crazy when they get older. You have this brain, still chugging along making things happen, but your body doesn't keep up and you can accept the inevitable or you can go nuts. Some of us accept. A lot of us go nuts. Quietly, but still, you can't call it anything else. It's crazy.

For example, I decided to tell the library girl the rest of the story. The whole thing. I was all hepped up to tell her more about my youthful indiscretion. Confession *was* proving to be good for the soul. My soul, anyway. It gave me kind of an energetic kick, especially after a week had passed with no visit from the constabulary.

I looked at everything a little differently. The swans seemed like the most beautiful and dazzling things in the universe. The cove shimmered and sparkled and glowed. My hands felt electric, like power was humming through them. I wanted to lift the world up and bury my face in it.

See what I say? Crazy thoughts.

Only thing, the library girl didn't come back the next week. They sent someone else. An older guy. Not old like me, but older than her. Fifty or something. I don't know. I was disappointed, to say the least.

Where's that sweet gal from last week? I asked.

He was all fake smiles and condescending tone. *Weeeeeeell*, he said, drawing out the word like it was a slug of taffy he was pulling, she's feeling just a *tiny* bit under the weather, he said. So they sent me in her place. Can I recommend a good book? I've got a nice western here for you.

A western. Did I look like I was wearing spurs and a cowboy hat? Did I look like I wanted to read about Indians and cowboys?

I turned around and shuffled off. I thought I knew what was going on. She was so put off by my confession that she couldn't stand the thought of coming back and spending time in my proximity. Couldn't blame her, I guess.

But here's the thing that I couldn't let go of: She didn't tell the police. No authorities came to question me. No one with a gun and handcuffs came to my door. So even though she knew about a terrible crime, she didn't report it. Which made her part of the lie now.

You can hardly know how much of a relief that was to me. Ever since the other two guys died, it had been a heavy burden on me, being the only one to know. It was like I was carrying around this overweight load of evil. Now, a small sliver of it had been shaved off and sprinkled on the library girl like a bit of devil's dust.

I did not believe for a second that she was feeling under the weather. That was a lie. She was afraid of me. Or afraid of herself, maybe. Sometimes it's hard to tell.

The next week, I was as surprised as anyone to see her back with her box of books for us decrepits. She spread them all out on the table in the great room and we all came over. Some of us by our own steam, some of us on wheelchairs. I came in and tried to catch her eye. She avoided me, though I could tell it was a fight. She *wanted* to look at me, only she thought it wouldn't be good for her. Not good for her soul to look at what she thought was evil.

You might think I exaggerate, but I don't. It was all there. She was afraid of me.

I waited until the rest of the residents had gone away and it was just the two of us in the great room.

I was sorry to hear you were not feeling well, I said.

Caught a bug, she said.

I'm not a bad man, I said.

You did a bad thing.

A long time ago.

She turned that over in her mind. I don't think that matters, she said.

Why did you come back?

It's my job.

The other guy could have come back. You didn't have to be here.

She thought about that for a long time. Longer than was healthy, if you ask me. It was like she was trying to redo the past, make it into something that didn't happen.

The other guy, she said. What did you think of him?

I shrugged. He seemed okay, I guess.

Her face darkened. It was strange, like I had said something even worse than before.

You don't think he's okay? I asked.

I'm not exactly comfortable around him, she said. He has a thing for me.

I could see it was hard for her to tell me.

Does he bother you? I asked.

She nodded. I kept thinking you were telling a story, she said. About killing someone. Not telling the truth. Was I right? Was it all just something you made up, like these murder stories? She held up a book with the picture of a bloody knife glistening on the cover.

No, I said. It's not a story. I really did it.

And you got away with it, she said. Wonder in her voice.

Yes I did, I said. Unless you turn me in.

She laughed. My great grandfather is your age, she said.

Do you think he did bad things when he was younger?

Probably. Doesn't everyone?

Have you? I asked.

She didn't answer. I couldn't tell if she wanted to or not.

Tell me, she said. Tell me what you did.

I thought of the murder books she had brought for us. People wanted to know about killers, didn't they? All kinds of people find some kind of joy in reading of such things. Who was I to deny her this indulgence?

You weren't far off when you asked me about the war, I said. It happened around that time. It was a couple of days after Pearl Harbor. You know what Pearl Harbor was, right?

She nodded. I'm not an idiot, she said.

No, I said, I suppose you're not. But lots of people from your generation don't know much about the past.

Tell me about the past, she said.

It was a time and a feeling in the air that hasn't been repeated. We thought the world was coming to an end, but at the same time, guys my age were excited. We wanted to join up and do our part. Me and two of my buddies, we decided we weren't going to wait to be drafted. We got together one day, shared a bottle of whiskey, just to get up the courage, and went down to the recruiting station. This was in Seattle. Along the way, we got to talking about what we were going to be getting into. We knew we were volunteering to kill other guys our age for our country. We were going to be trained to be killers. But, you know, it's not a long way to go for some of us. My buddies, they were the kind of guys who got into fights all the time. Liked to pound on other guys. We talked about what it would mean to kill. I wasn't sure I could do it. My buddies said it would be easy. They were looking forward to killing Japs. Or Krauts. It didn't matter to them. Or to a lot of guys. Recruiting offices had lines at their doors blocks long. The country was *ready* to kill.

But I was not like that. I did not have murder in my heart. Not at first. I told them again, I just didn't know if I had it in me. They told me I was going to be trained. The army knew how to turn guys into killers. Even *we* know how to do that, said one of them.

I'm not going to blame the whiskey. Or the influence of my peers. It was a strange time and what happened next seems like someone else's story. But it's not. It's my story.

It was about ten in the morning. Typical December in Seattle: wet and cold. It wasn't exactly raining, but it wasn't dry, either. Our hair and faces were wet from droplets hanging in the air. We passed people on the sidewalk who nodded at us and smiled at us. It was like they knew where we were going: we were about to sign up and fight for the country. It was patriotic and we felt *good*. Really good.

We were a couple of blocks from the recruiting station. We saw a line already there. Guys our age. We whooped and hollered, feeling that rush of community, you know, when you find your tribe? You ever feel that?

The library gal nodded. I think so, she said.

If you ever did, I said, you'd know it. Not thinking about it. I don't know if your generation has that anymore. You're all too separate now, with your computers and your cell phones. You don't have that tribal feeling.

She cleared her throat. You were saying?

She wanted more of the story. I couldn't tell if she hoped it would be awful or not as bad as she already thought it was. I made no editorial comments on my narrative. I just plunged on.

We were hugging each other, there on the sidewalk, after seeing all the other guys and then we started running the last few blocks to get there quicker. We wanted to be part of something. Something bigger than us.

Then this guy, this small guy, he stepped out from nowhere, from an alley, from between two buildings, and he was holding up a sign in front of us that he'd painted. He held it up high. It said WAR IS MURDER.

I've thought about him a lot over the years. He had his convictions, everyone does. But he didn't keep it to himself, which is what most people do. In a climate of fevered agreement on the need for war, he stepped out in front of three guys gunning for war, and told them they were doing something wrong.

At first we didn't care. We started to step around him, but he stepped to the side, blocking our way.

Understand, he was a small man. It was nothing for us to step around him, but.

But.

One of my buddies stopped and looked him right in the eye. You don't want to get in our way, he said to the guy with the sign.

Don't be killers, said the man.

My buddy tilted his head to me. All of us had stopped. Did you hear that? Guy says we shouldn't be killers. What you think of that? He was asking me. Wanting an opinion? Not exactly. More like wanting me to say the guy was nuts. He *was* nuts, let's face it. Even if he was right, he was crazy insane to step in front of three guys on a mission like we were.

Let it go, I said.

No, said my buddy. I don't think so. I think maybe this is where our training starts. So then my buddy, he grabbed the guy's sign out of his hands and tossed it down to the sidewalk and I could tell the small guy was scared. He was shaking, but he didn't back away.

I don't want you young men turning into killers, he said.

What do you care? I said.

I'm a pacifist.

I hardly knew what the word meant back then. He was a guy who didn't believe in violence. I could respect that. I told my friends to leave him and let's go.

But my buddy, the guy I had allied myself with, he made a fist, drew it back and punched the guy in the stomach. The guy bent over, coughing. His face was red and he put out his arms, reaching for something to hold him up that wasn't there.

Come on, I said. He's an old guy. Leave him alone. But then my other friend, he leaned close to me. The guy's a low life, he said. He's against the country. He wants the Japs to win.

No, I said. That's not true.

But my other friend, by this time, he had grabbed the guy and pulled him into the alley from where he came. My friend threw the guy on the pavement. His head hit hard. I heard something crack.

A shot of adrenaline laced through me. I wanted us out of there, but I couldn't leave them. Couldn't just run out on my friends.

They grabbed his arms and dragged him even further into the alley. He moaned a few times. Just sounds. No voice in him anymore. It was dark in there. No lights and the sun was just a blurry gray patch in the clouds.

Okay, I said. Let's leave him here. We taught him a lesson.

But that didn't stop anything. They both kicked him in the ribs. One after the other. He writhed on the ground. My friends looked at me. Now you, they said.

I took a breath and let it out. No, I said.

Do you agree with him?

No!

Are you one of us?

I waited.

Waited for someone to come into the alley and we would scatter. Waited for the guy to get up and pull away into a corner. Waited for a fairy godmother to swoop down and make him better and send us on our way. Waited for what seemed a very long time.

I heard his feet and hands scrape against the ground like he was trying to grab something. Reaching. The sound of it, like rats clawing at walls, it changed something in me. I just wanted the guy to stop making noise. Any noise. I wanted the quiet of the world to come back and help me.

Lives turn on moments. A split second and everything changes. They were my friends. They wanted something from me. I decided I would give them what they wanted.

Yes, I said.

Then I pulled back my foot and aimed it at the guy's head and kicked for all I was worth.

Here's the awful thing. It felt good. I wanted to kick him. Hard. So I did it again. I could see his head was pretty banged up. Blood was spilling out of him. Soon the three of us were like a machine, the pistons of our feet working him over from head to toe. I'm not sure when exactly he died.

When we were done, we walked out of there and never talked about it again. We went to war, did our time. Never killed anyone while we were in service. Funny thing is, the military did make us better people. Better men. More compassionate, I think. More considerate of others. Attentive to duty. Champions of the weak. They were just a day late for that poor guy who got in the way of the wrong recruits.

Lots of times I thought about that morning. What we did. What I did. I felt guilty, but not guilty enough to turn myself in. The last few years, the memories of what we did that morning, they've been coming back stronger and stronger. And now, here I am telling you.

The library gal had been listening very attentively the whole time. When I was finished, that churchy silence came back. It lasted for a long time.

That man, she said. You never paid the price for his death. You lived a long life.

I nodded. That I did.

Which was all he wanted for you. He just wanted you to live a long life and not kill people.

That's right.

She shook her head. My story was worse than she had imagined it would be.

I don't know what to do now, she said.

You don't have to do anything.

Yes, she said. Yes, I do.

Panic gripped me. But only momentarily. I said earlier that I didn't want the police to take me away. That changed after I told the whole story to her. Now that it was out, really out, I had this peculiar feeling come over me, like I decided I needed to pay. Not a lot. But some. A little. I should maybe go to jail for the rest of my life. That wasn't going to be a lot of years anyway.

The library gal, she stared me in the eye and I stared right back at her. You do what you have to do, I said.

I will, she said.

Then she got her books together and was gone in a few minutes.

I spent the rest of the day in a daze. I sat in the great room, staff and inmates milling around me, going about their business, barely noticing that I was on the verge of tears for hours on end, thinking my life was over.

Crying is supposed to be good for the soul, too. Like confession. I didn't see it that way.

Three days after I told my story to the library gal, I was in my room, dozing, when a sharp rapping on my door woke me up to the world.

Come in, I said.

The door swung open. It was just as I had envisioned it. Two officers stood in the doorway, dark silhouettes against the fluorescent hallway lights.

Yes? I said.

They came inside and stood over me, like they were taking up positions to pummel me senseless.

We have some questions for you, they said.

Yes?

You recently had contact with an employee from the library?

I talked to her, yes.

She says if we talk to you, we'll understand everything.

Everything? I said.

The young lady has been charged with murder, said one of the officers. She says she got the idea from you. Any idea what she's talking about?

My world flipped over on itself. It was a good thing I was lying down, because otherwise I would have toppled to the floor from the dizziness that wrapped me up at that moment.

Murder? I said.

Accomplice, actually. We think she hired someone to kill a guy who's been stalking her. She doesn't deny it, but we need to know a little more. She says you gave her the idea that she could get away with it. Is there something we should know, sir? Is there something you need to tell us?

I destroyed one life a long time ago. Then, on the eve of my own demise, I destroyed another. Not such good bookends for a life that had been very good to me. I swallowed hard. Those tears, those damned tears, rose up in me again. I wanted to take it all back. Wanted to keep the story to myself. Wished I had never told her. Wished I never needed to confess.

Officers, I said. I'm sorry to hear about what this poor girl did, but I tell you, I don't know where she got the idea. Certainly not from me. I'm a frail old man, waiting to die.

About the Author

MARIO MILOSEVIC LIVES in the Pacific Northwest. His stories have appeared in *Alfred Hitchcock's Mystery Magazine, Fiction River, Interzone, Asimov's SF,, The Magazine of Fantasy and Science Fiction,* and many others. His novels include *The Last Giant, Kyle's War,* and *The Coma Monologues.* Learn more at mariowrites.com.